# ZELLE

## SISTER WITCHES OF STORY COVE SPELLBINDING COZY MYSTERY SERIES, BOOK 5

### NYX HALLIWELL

Beach Path Publishing, LLC

Zelle, Sister Witches of Story Cove Spellbinding Cozy Mystery Series, Book 5

©2020; 2022 Nyx Halliwell

Re-release date December 6, 2022

*Previously published as Hexed Hair Day*

Print: 978-1-948686-73-0

Cover by Fanderclai Design **www.fanderclai.com**

CHAPTER

# ONE

As midnight approaches, silence wraps around the Enchanted shop. The house, too, is quiet, except for Elvis crooning *Blue Christmas* in the background, as the candy cane soap I've made hardens in a bright red mold.

It's the happiest time of the year, according to most people. For me? Not so much. Don't get me wrong—I have a terrific family, I love my dual jobs here at the candle and soap company, as well as the salon, and I enjoy a good life. I'm luckier than many, but I don't have two very important things I desperately long for—my parents, and the man I love.

My phone dings on the work table and I catch the notification that I have four matches on Fairytale Love, the dating app I use for distraction. I've set up multiple accounts, each with their own profile, and none that state I'm a beauty witch, or that my hair grows six feet a day.

The local bachelors all know me and most swipe left, passing me by, regardless of my glowing hair and smiling profile photos. I've already dated the single men in town anyway. The fact there are four who've swiped right today means they're desperate for a date to an office Christmas party or just plain lonely.

I sympathize. It's hard to be single during the holidays. "Sing it, King," I tell Elvis, as he insists the red and green decorations aren't the same without his love to share them with.

The guy I fell for in middle school is long gone. I haven't heard from him in nearly four years.

And while my sisters miss our parents, the gap left by their deaths is a raw hole of emotion that I fall down every year when autumn comes around. Halloween, Thanksgiving, Christmas...those special days never seem right without them here.

Christmas is also the time of the year that reminds me of Sawyer the most. Before he and I broke up on Christmas Eve, we both loved the season with its trees, lights, and songs. It really was the happiest time of year for me then. Now, I can't look at a decoration or wrapping paper without thinking of him.

Of course, I have to keep all of this from my sisters, pretending everything is great, and that I'm as excited as they are about the season. My twin, Belle, especially loves it, and this one is extra special for her. Because she does such a great job with the fall book fair every year, the Chamber of Commerce has asked her to also handle the downtown Christmas festival.

Luckily, the candle and soap business is so busy with holiday shoppers, I barely have time to catch my breath. We each have our responsibilities running Enchanted, and mine is the sales floor three afternoons a week. I also fill online orders. Along with the hours here, my stylist skills are in high demand. I'm booked with hair and makeup appointments through to the new year.

Cinder, the oldest, has recently installed a small but efficient commercial kitchen as part of a remodel project we're doing. By opening up our backroom and rearranging the work and storage areas, we now have more square footage for merchandise and this upgraded kitchen.

While the pretty new quartz countertops come in handy when we're creating products, this space is Ruby's domain. She's second age-wise, and is a fabulous cook and healer. Her line of candies are sold all over town and have gained a near-cult following. Both Story Cove residents, as well as our growing tourist population, order larger and larger quantities every week. I personally love the hot cocoa truffles with peppermint chips on top.

Recently, I've been using the kitchen as much as she has. I'm a terrible cook, but I'm a decent witch. Once she's in bed, I experiment with our grandmother Eunice's spell books and potions, searching for one to mend my broken heart.

Our fourth great-grandmother built Enchanted, and kept recipes of every type of soap, candle, and lotion she created and sold. She also wrote about her daily life in journals. We recently discovered a treasure trove of these documents hidden in a secret room in the mansion's turret.

She was kind of obsessive with her collection of books and her day-by-day diaries, but I'm glad for their contents. While Ruby's enjoyed reading her journals and a pile of love letters between her and Ezra, our grandfather, Belle has dived into the editions on local history and magick. For me, I've been studying them for medicinal brews, tinctures, and tonics. Along with keeping her dream alive, the four of us Sherwood sisters inherited her love for white magick.

Elvis fades off and Bing takes his place, assuring me he'll be home for Christmas. My father's favorite song. I imagine him standing here at the stove with me, booming out the words, and teasing me about my love life. He always believed I'd have a dozen suitors one day.

I scan the four potentials, sighing at the familiar names. *Yep, office parties and loneliness for the win.*

I've dated plenty of guys since Sawyer left, even throwing myself into this find-true-love app, determined to do just that, but it hasn't worked. My heart was stolen when I was eleven, and I never got it back.

After I'm done cooking this potion to help me get over him once and for all, maybe I'll watch White Christmas and keep pretending Dad is here. He and Mom always sang along to all the movie's tunes, and I'd give anything to hear their voices once more.

I hum along with Bing as I gather the last of the ingredients and stir. In the overhead light, the strand of Sawyer's hair is midnight black as I hold it up to examine it. I discovered it two days ago on a scarf buried in a drawer. His grandmother sewed the garment for me, the fabric covered in cartoonish ferrets. My ferret familiar, Rumpelstiltskin, plays with a toy in the corner of the room, his thin, furry body as supple and fluid as an acrobat's.

I drop the strand into the bubbling potion and watch the liquid change from a translucent yellow to a mint green. Eunice's spell claims the concoction needs to cook for twenty minutes, then cool for twenty-four hours, before I drink it.

*Twenty-four hours.* Will my heart finally be healed before Christmas?

"Insomnia again?"

I jump at the sound of Ruby's voice, and wheel around to find her yawning as she enters the room. Her familiar, a raven named Lenore, flies in and perches on the chair in the corner. My sister doesn't wait for an answer as she eyes the loaf of candy cane soap. "I love the sparkle effect on top. Is it set?"

The playlist switches to a modern rendition of Silent Night. *Sure isn't one for me.* Hastily, I close the book and try to block the pot from her sight with my body. "Should be. I'll cut it before I go to bed."

"I can do it." She turns the product out of the form and onto the table before she grabs the slicer. "I put the kettle on for tea, if you want to talk about anything."

The red and white striped loaf falls into neat rectangle-shaped bars as she cuts. A few flakes of glitter scatter over the countertop. "What's to talk about?" I fiddle with the end of my braid. "Sometimes I can't sleep, it's no big deal. You really should go back to bed. I need to hit the sack, too. Big day tomorrow with the Stevenson wedding."

"Zelle?" Ruby gives me a funny look as she sets down the cutter. "What's up with your hair?"

A rainbow of colors play across her face, like LED lights. Lenore caws, her tiny head turning from side to side as she stares at me.

My tresses are directly tied to my magick, and tonight, I've wrapped the thick plait twice around my waist, and the tip still drags the ground. I glance down to see it glowing brightly. Colors flow down the tendrils in waves—blue, purple, green, yellow, orange, and red. A fresh kaleidoscope follows on the heels of the last. This time, it's a monotone of pinks, from raspberry to the palest pastel.

I can change the color at will, which I love doing, but I'm not causing this display. "Holy highlights," I whisper. "I don't know."

Ruby glances around me at the pot and sees the book. Her eyes narrow. "Are you experimenting with Eunice's potions again? Must be some strong magick to cause that."

She points at my hair as Cinder enters with her standard bedhead. She's dressed in flannel pjs with hedgehogs on them, and her own pygmy hedgehog, McAlister, is in the crook of her arm. His whiskers twitch, either at the various aromas in the air or my psychedelic mane. "What's going on?"

*Distract them!* I point to the sliced bars on the counter. "I made candy cane soaps."

"And something else," Ruby adds, cautiously sniffing at the steam over the pot. She checks the end of a lock, but nothing happens to it and she glances at mine again. "Zelle's having a reaction to it, I think."

This could go all shades of wrong and very quickly, and I don't mean just the color of my hair. My older sisters already worry too much about me. I can't let them know I'm doing this to get over Sawyer. I mean, it's been four years. I should be long over him, right?

"It's only a new wash," I lie, waving off their concern. "With the winter air, my strands need lots of moisture. Eunice has plenty of potions for nourishing dry, split ends. I'm experimenting with a few."

Both sisters eye me with clear skepticism and a touch of suspicion. Since I have to shave my hair daily due to its ridiculous growth rate, there's no reason for me to use fancy shampoos or conditioners. "Is your magick all right?" Ruby asks.

"Sure. Fine." I glimpse the varied and brilliant colors rippling past my nose. "It's, um, actually for a client." Always a good excuse. "I'm testing it on myself first, you know, to be sure it's safe."

This is more plausible, but I see the glance they exchange. Cinder shifts McAlister and assumes her head of the family stance with feet planted and a composed expression. "Whatever's going on, Zelle, you can tell us."

They're not buying my lie, and I can't blame them. "Nothing is going on. I like potions, you know that, and Eunice has a good deal of them. I simply want to play a little, okay? I swear, I'm fine, and this" I flip my braid over my shoulder, "is probably due to stress more than anything else. It's a busy time of year and we're all feeling it."

Another silent exchange passes between them.

Ruby pats my shoulder. "We're not trying to irritate you, we just worry. You have a lot on your plate."

"As do both of you, but we're Sherwoods." I purposely look each of them in the eye. "We may not have fairytale lives like Momma wanted for us, but we know how to rise above the crummy stuff and keep on going."

Cinder winks at me and sets McAlister on the floor to toddle off. "Agreed. However, I want your promise that if you need to talk, you'll say so."

The eldest of us, she's carried the mother mantle since our parents' deaths. It hasn't been easy, and I feel guilty for making her worry. Ruby, too. "I promise," I tell her, more to make her feel better than to wrap up this uncomfortable conversation.

"Oh good." Belle enters, as bright-eyed and wide-awake as any of us. The woman could go days without sleep and never show it, and it's all due to her sunny disposition. "You're all here."

My playlist switches again, restarting Elvis.

My twin has brought a tray of drinks—Santa mugs filled with cocoa and candy canes—and sets it on the end of the work table. The Santas are all winking and giving a devil-may-care smile, as if they've just filled our stockings with everything we wished for. She takes a seat on one of the stools, slides a notebook out from under the tray, and begins handing out the drinks. She does a double take at my hair. "I like it. Very festive."

She always has my back and doesn't jump to the

assumption anything is wrong. I love that about her. "Thank you." I raise a defiant chin to the others.

She shifts the notebook, which goes everywhere with her these days. She's decorated it with Christmas stickers and a red and green plaid ribbon to mark her spot. "I want to go over your assignments for the Christmas in Story Cove Festival next week. We have a lot to do to prepare."

Cinder is reaching to accept a mug and her hand freezes in midair. "Assignments?" She looks as though she might run from the room.

Belle's Pekingese, Jayne, hops into her favorite chair near the front window and settles. Rumpelstiltskin joins her and curls up against her, burying his nose under his own tail, so he looks like a fur ball.

Savannah, our shop cat is in her bed in the window seat and she peeks at them with a sniff. As long as they aren't bothering her, she decides they can stay. She stretches and closes her eyes again.

Belle pointedly hands Cinder her cup and waits for her to concede and accept it. "You know I'm in charge this year, and I'm up to my tinsel in preparations. I need all of you to participate and help me out."

Her organizational skills may top Cinder's. She and I are twins, but fraternal ones, and I am her opposite in lots of ways. Belle likes rules and organization, I resist both. She's perpetually upbeat, and sees the best in everyone and everything. I'm more likely to see the clouds than the silver lining. She's Miss Social Butterfly—I only interact with folks because I want to do their hair and makeup. It's an art form for me and my magick, and I'm compelled to play.

Ruby wanders over, taking a mug and stirring the cocoa with the candy cane. "I can't wait for the downtown walk. I'm helping Ren decorate his front window."

I lower the stove flame and turn off the music. "Sorry, sis, but I'm already overbooked with clients and I have a waiting list."

She dismisses my statement with a flip of the notebook as she peruses the written details inside. "You're in charge of the hair and makeup of the theater cast." She looks up and smiles, ignoring my mumbled dissension. "We're doing The Night Before Christmas at the outdoor amphitheater. Won't that be fun?"

I attempt to reason with her, but she raises a hand as a stop sign, turning a page. "Cinder, the stage needs work. There are loose boards and two sections of the roof leak. We need it fixed and the sound systems checked. Feel free to recruit volunteers to help you." From a pocket in the back of the notebook, she produces a loose paper. "Here's the complete list. The Chamber will reimburse any expenses you incur."

Cinder would rather have a hammer in her hand than pretty much anything else. Still, she looks disappointed. "I'd love to pitch in, Belle, but—"

"No buts." Belle glares at all of us. At our silence, she runs a finger down her bulleted list. "Christmas comes once a year. It's been a hard twelve months for this town, and we all deserve holiday cheer. The festival guarantees folks joy and happiness. You've been working hard, Cinder." She meets our sister's eyes once more. "We all have. The shop remodel is progressing nicely and sales are up. We'd all work twenty-four-seven if we could to build our empire, but we're part of this community. They support us, and it's time to give back."

It's a rare thing for any of us to chastise Cinder, and the silence continues for a long, pregnant moment. She frowns at Belle then sighs, accepting the list begrudgingly. "I'll get Finn to help me."

Cinder's boyfriend is like Belle, a total social butterfly, and he's handy to have around, too. He makes Cinder go out and do things she normally would resist, and he makes her happy, which is all I care about.

Belle brightens considerably. "Good. And I'm sure there are others who will lend a hand."

"What about me?" Ruby asks. She has a bit of cocoa on her top lip. "How can I help?"

"You're in charge of the gingerbread house and cookie competition." Belle sips her drink and hands Ruby another sheaf of paper. "We're doing separate adult and children's contests. We already have a dozen entrants for the houses, and even more for the cookie contest." She peers around to make sure we're alone. "Don't tell Matilda or she'll want to enter."

Our godmother is almost as bad a cook as I am, and I burn toast. Recently, she's been watching a foodie cable channel and experimenting with various recipes. When she puts a spell on the stove, some actually turn out all right, but the others... I shudder remembering the runny, disgusting spinach quiche she served last week. I'm never eating spinach again.

"Awesome." Ruby sets down her mug to take the list and scan it. "What exactly do I have to do?"

"First, you'll need to select a panel of judges."

"I volunteer."

Belle startles at Matilda's voice. Our godmother saunters in dressed like she's ready for a date rather than bed. Her glittery makeup makes me cringe, and her purple outfit is straight out of the 1960s. At least her hair is holding the curls I magicked into it earlier today. "I love cookies and I have a very discerning palate."

Ruby winks at Belle, whose shoulders sag with relief at the fact she isn't entering the contest. "You're hired," Ruby says.

The last of our group joins us as Uncle Odin shuffles in, tying the belt of his dark duster. His robe is covered in dog hair from Jayne and he's left off his eye patch. His white hair sticks out in all directions, resembling Einstein's. "What about me, dear?" He picks up the cocoa meant for me and drinks, leaving a coating on his white mustache. "I'm more than happy to assist, if you can use an old man like me."

Belle smiles at the stain. His beard, a match for his hair, seems longer than usual, and I realize I've been so caught up in my world, I've forgotten to trim it.

"Gordon Digs fell in his bathtub yesterday and broke his hip. We need a Santa Claus."

Uncle Odin's glee matches that of a child's on Christmas morning. "You wish me to play St. Nick?"

Belle nods.

"I shall endeavor to do a good job, then."

"You're perfect for the part," I assure him.

Belle takes a sip of her cocoa. "We'll also need you at the open house to fill the role with the kids. You'll need to listen to their requests and have your photo taken with them."

He beams. "How nice."

Ruby rubs his arm. "They'll love you. Some of them are already convinced you're Santa."

"I can be your helpful Mrs. Claus," Matilda offers. "I'll dig up that costume from three years ago. Remember, I won second place in the contest at Gloria Simpson's party with it? Would have gotten first if Lucinda Culpepper hadn't come as Britney Spears and did a karaoke rendition of her greatest hits." She rolls her eyes.

I press my lips together so I don't laugh. Matilda is no singer, and the judges are lucky she didn't break out in her version of *Rocking Around the Christmas Tree*.

Always a gentleman, Uncle Odin smiles at her. "You're number one with me, my dear."

She wraps her arms around his neck and hugs him. "Ditto, St. Nick."

We've all been so scattered, it's the first time in

weeks we've gathered together as a family. It makes me relax and my hair does, too.

Putting an arm around Belle's shoulder, I squeeze, pushing away the sadness I feel. She, Ruby, and Cinder have all found true love this year, and who knows what the future will bring? Marriages and children, I expect.

Meanwhile, I'll be here at Enchanted forever, with Uncle Odin and Matilda, and maybe that's for the best. My dreams of a Christmas Eve wedding and a life with Sawyer were never meant to be.

Shoving the pain and disappointment into that deep hole once more, I paste on a matching smile to Belle's. "When do we start?"

CHAPTER

# THREE

That weekend I make it through the Stevenson's wedding preparations without any issues. The only problem I have is my hair and its continuing ridiculous bouts of rainbow colors. Although plenty of folks know I'm a witch and assume I'm doing it on purpose, the out of town guests who catch sight of it give me odd stares. I ignore them and skedaddle as soon as the bridal march sounds.

Since I drank the potion, I feel more cheerful and less worried about being swamped by emotions over the coming days. I toyed with the four matches on the dating app, but eventually passed on all of them. Belle's got plenty to keep me busy when I'm not doing my regular client's hair and makeup or working at the shop, and I don't want to be arm bling for anyone at an office party get-together. Besides, how embarrassing for both of us if my hair wigs out.

Maybe Eunice knew a thing or two about heart-break, and if her remedy gets me through this week, I'm grateful. I'll drink a gallon of it to keep the blues away. My only concern is what's causing my continual bad hair days. Is it an ingredient or something else?

Monday morning, it's before opening time at the shop and I'm on the phone with a supplier as I restock shelves. We're out of our favorite soy blend candle wax and I'm hoping I can get some overnighted. The holiday rush has depleted our hottest candle—Christmas Hearth—and we need more for this week.

Belle returns from her morning run to the bank and unwraps her scarf as the supplier tells me they are sold out of the needed wax. I hang up, disappointed and frustrated. "No deal. Every one of our usual wholesalers is out."

She opens the cash drawer and refills the various slots. A roll of quarters cracks against the metal side and coins clink as they fall in. "What about the candle shop in Clover Hills? The one Kathleen runs. Maybe they have stock we can buy."

I give her a thumbs-up. "Brilliant. Why didn't I think of that?"

"You would have." She taps her temple. "I've been problem-solving all month for the festival, so my brain is hyperactive right now, but it's good to know you still need me once in a while."

"Always," I tell her, giving her a quick hug.

I look up the number and call. While I wait for the gal who answers to hunt down the owner, I return to the storeroom and load up the rolling cart with Candy Cane soaps, Silver Bell bath bombs, and Cinder's North lotion that smells like pine trees and peppermint. It's one of her new lines of pain-relieving products, and folks love it because they don't smell like typical medicinal salves.

Kathleen answers. "Hi, Zelle. Merry Christmas. How can I help you?"

I explain our dilemma, crossing my fingers.

"Happy to do you a favor, if I can," she says. "Give me a minute to check."

Filtered Christmas music comes over the line. I wheel the full cart to the showroom. Matilda is sweeping the floor and humming to Belle's Christmas playlist. Her full skirt is tiered in bright holiday colors and she's made a set of earrings to match. While I'm not wild about the skirt, I do like the earrings. "Pretty," I say, pointing at them. She smiles, sets the broom aside and takes the cart from me. I wander aimlessly around as she begins restocking shelves.

"Zelle?" Kathleen returns. "We have six pounds that we can part with. I know it's not much, but it's all I can manage. Would you like to pick it up today?"

"That would be great." I consider my schedule and which appointments I'll need to rearrange. "We really appreciate it."

"I'll have it ready for you. By the way, I'd love some of your fairytale bath products. Just for me—I deserve a treat, and I've heard a lot about them."

"I'd be happy to bring you some."

"Then the wax is on the house. Merry Christmas."

Relieved, I promise to bring her a big bag full of our popular products. "And to you."

After I hang up, I calculate my time crunch. "It's thirty minutes each way to Clover Hills." I study the calendar notations on my phone app. "I'll have to cancel Nonni's cut, and hurry back before Clara Tildings' wash and curl. I sure hope traffic is light."

"You better hope Nonni doesn't have Santa put coal in your stocking," Belle chastises.

I bite my lower lip. "I hate to let her down, but I have to get the wax, make the candles, and let them cure, all today. Plus, I have six internet orders for Christmas Hearth as well."

"I can pick up the wax," Matilda volunteers.

Cinder will kill me for letting her drive the shop van, but if she runs the errand, it will save me a lot of stress and keep our grandmother happy.

You do not want to be on Nonni's bad side.

"You're a lifesaver." I stuff half a dozen of the requested fairytale products in a bag and throw in a few Candy Cane soaps. I'd rather deal with Cinder's disapproval than Nonni's.

"I'll take Odin, unless you need him here," our godmother offers. "He hasn't been out of the house in days."

Belle assures her she can handle the shop and Matilda fills a thermos with eggnog. I help Uncle Odin into the van.

"How are you feeling?" he asks out of the blue.

Matilda shoots us both a look as she buckles in.

"I'm fine," I tell him. "You two have fun."

He grabs my arm before I can shut the door. "You're a good girl, Zelle."

I'm not sure what this is about, but I kiss his cheek. "Thanks, Santa."

When I return inside, Belle is getting ready to unlock the front door. "What did you get Cinder for Christmas?"

"This three-in-one tool Finn told me about. She was eyeing it at the hardware store. You?"

"New work boots. I hope she likes them. You know how picky she is about her footwear."

"What about Ruby?"

She smiles, obviously proud of this gift. "A subscription to an online baking school! It has hundreds of videos for candy making. She's going to love it. I thought she could get some new ideas for her business."

"That's cool." I return the cart to the back and find Rumpelstiltskin batting at a silicone soap mold. He balks when I take it away from him, but promptly steals Jayne's favorite stuffed squirrel and the two dash upstairs to continue playtime. Savannah sniffs and saunters out to the showroom and her window bed.

"What about you?" Belle asks when I return. "What did you get Ruby?"

I motion her over and remove a business card from my back pocket. "Do you think she'll like them?"

"Sweet On You Confections," Belle reads. This is the name Ruby has chosen for her business. "Oh Zelle, they're beautiful."

I admire the vintage Victorian font and decorative border, reminiscent of an old-time candy shop. "I really hope she'll take the plunge and rent the empty store space next to Ren's clinic."

Ruby's boyfriend is the town veterinarian and between his building and the quilt shop is an empty retail slot that would be perfect for her. Of course, that would mean she would have fewer hours at Enchanted, but this is her chance to do something else she really loves. I think she should go for it.

There's a rumbling in the distance. Belle frowns. "You want her to leave us?"

The weather is supposed to be cold but not stormy. I glance toward the window and see it's cloud-free. "It's two blocks, Belle. The space is small but ideal for a sweet shop. Plus, Matilda wants to sell her jewelry designs and Nonni is always at the quilt shop whenever she gets a chance. They can help her run it. If Ruby really wants to branch out, I think she should."

"Says the sister who wants her own beauty salon."

I don't, but I'd sure like to create haircare products, including natural color dyes. "Says the sister who wants to buy the bookstore."

Belle sucks in a breath and looks shocked. "You know?"

I put an arm around her shoulders. "You still believe you can keep secrets from me? From any of us?

You'll sell that romance novel of yours one of these days, buy Beanstalk Books, and live happily ever after."

She pinches my side. "You're incorrigible. Did Leo tell you?"

"He's innocent. You have a brilliant mind, sister, but I can always read it." I wink at her. "By the way, I don't want my own place. I'd be perfectly happy to work with clients here. Cinder and I are still talking about that, but finishing the main remodel comes first."

"I have this dream," she says, wistfully. "We could connect Enchanted with the bookstore via a covered walkway. Folks wouldn't have to even go outside. And we could have displays in both shops that highlight books and products. Just like now, we could have an arrangement of our Christmas soaps with holiday stories. Our Library Afternoon candles would be a perfect fit for literary classics, and our fairytale line with—"

"Fairytales, I get it. Sounds wonderful."

The rumble grows louder—not thunder, must be an approaching vehicle. Main Street doesn't allow semi-trucks but I realize it's not coming from one of those.

In fact, I recognize that noise. *A motorcycle.*

Swiftly, I move to the window. Belle joins me. Together we lean to stare down the road. There are a few die-hard riders this time of year, but few who will brave the cold and often icy conditions. We're far enough south in Georgia we don't often get snow, but we still have winter weather.

The deep-throated rumble of the bike fills the air as it glides slowly past our shop. All of my good cheer puddles at my feet.

"Is that who I think it is?" my twin asks hesitantly.

I walk out the door, onto the sidewalk, watching the bike and the man on it. He's in leather from head to toe, mirrored sunglasses covering his eyes, reflecting the morning sun back to me.

I swallow hard as he wheels into the parking spot in front of Quilting Quarters and eases off the seat. My blood slams through my veins making my pulse jump. *It can't be.*

Belle joins me, rubbing her arms against the cold. "Zelle...?"

The man must sense us watching him. His head turns our direction.

With an *eep* of recognition, Belle whirls so she's shielding me. Her eyes, so like mine, bore into my frozen gaze. "Time to go back inside."

Over her shoulder, I watch the owner of the quilt shop fly out the front door. She squeals, the sound echoing down the street. "You're home!"

The man hugs her, lifting her off the ground, but I can't hear his reply. My heart is beating so hard, it drowns him out.

"Zelle, snap out of it. I'm freezing. Come on."

As Belle tugs me toward the entrance, my legs feel

leaden. "Sorry..." I say feebly, the emotions I believed were gone flooding through me once again.

I not only see the rainbow colors flash through my growing hair, I *feel* them. Red for anger, orange for desire, yellow for courage. Just before we're through the door, I glance over my shoulder at the reunion still taking place down the street. Minerva is beside herself with joy.

The sunglasses are gone, and before I can look away, Sawyer Wilden catches me watching. He raises a hand as though to wave.

"Merry Christmas," he calls, his voice a silvery rustle on the wind.

# FOUR

After four years, the guy who broke my heart is back in town to visit his grandmother. I knew it would happen someday, yet I'm not prepared.

My ten o'clock, Deanna Reiner, is full of gossip. As I highlight her hair, the drone of her voice is like background Christmas music—I barely register it. I keep my focus solely on sectioning the tresses, painting on the solution, and wrapping each in foil.

Unfortunately, the reflective square shows me a distorted version of my face, reminding me of Sawyer's sunglasses.

"You used to be sweet on him, didn't you?"

The question jerks me out on my melancholy. "Sorry?"

"Sawyer—he's back in town. Still single, I heard." She winks at me in the mirror.

I stutter for a moment. "That's nice." I then steer

the conversation to other topics—her family's Christmas gathering, the Story Cove events this week.

She tips generously, since it's the season, and I add it to my stash. I've been saving all of them to give to Belle for the bookstore purchase. Her boss, Daisy, is in on it, working out a deal with me. So far, I've gathered enough for a down payment, if Belle chooses to go for her dream.

My share of profits goes to the remodeling fund. I force my mind off Sawyer and take care of my clients with the hopes of adding to both stockpiles generously this week.

Next up for weddings is the Beaumont ceremony. Weddings definitely pay better than the daily clientele. Anna is having a simple Christmas Eve celebration at the arboretum a few miles east of town, with a casual, no fuss observance. I only need to style her, her matron of honor, and her mother, Charlene.

Unfortunately, Char wants to change Anna's already chosen beachy-wave look that we plan to allow to cascade down her back. Instead, she's insisting I devise a formal bun with a tiara. The two women enter the shop arguing and square off over my chair without coming up for air.

"But Mom!" Anna's face is three shades of angry pink. The photo she's printed from the internet of what she wants crinkles in her hand. "It's MY wedding. I want romantic and mermaid-ish, like my dress, not traditional and uptight!"

Her mother's face is mottled, as well, and her eyes

snap with vexation. "You'll thank me later when you see how perfect the updo and crystals will look. Besides, I'm paying for this, I should get what I want, too."

The owner of the salon, Glenda, motions at me to resolve this quickly and quietly. Replays of this public argument will top gossip hour all over town later today.

My schedule is packed and I have a perm client already waiting in the black and white decorated reception area. She and several others look on with rapt attention.

"How about a compromise?" I suggest. "We can do a half-up half-down, like this." I use my fingers to section Anna's long hair into pieces, winding one of them around and pinning it up quick as can be. Then I hastily work on the rest as I continue. "We can braid this section, weave in a few crystals to match the tiara, and leave the braid to cascade over the shoulder. Add the tiara, and voila."

I turn Anna to face the mirror. "Of course, it will be more polished the day of the wedding," I explain, "but this style is glamorous and still beachy."

Her eyes widen, and her mother nods, studying the effect. Anna touches her fingers to the bare side of her neck. Her diamond earring flashes in the light. "It brings out my eyes."

"I love it," her mom says. "It shows off your gorgeous shoulders."

Problem solved, I assure both of them that Anna

will be stunning, no matter what she decides to do, and then walk them to the door.

Glenda nods and I welcome my scheduled client.

"I can't wait for the tree lighting tomorrow night," Paige Willoughby says. "It's my favorite part of the downtown festivities."

There are two large fir trees flanking City Hall. Each year, the chamber and a host of volunteers decorate one with giant ornaments and multicolored lights. The second has been designated the angel tree, and people write wishes on ribbons to hang on the branches.

The topper is a serene angel made by a local artisan. The figurine has long, flowing locks in silver, white, and gold. When I was a child, my mother told me the artist was inspired by my hair and designed it after me.

I miss my mother and her stories, and these days, my locks are generally tinted in various bright colors, thanks to my magick. I still haven't figured out why my mane is radiating rainbows right now, but it's probably because I've been playing with so many of Eunice's potions. "I enjoy it, too," I say honestly. "I'll see you there."

An unexpected client in my book is Ren's cousin, Marion Rainhart Redfern. He prefers Rainhart, and friends call him Rain. "This is a nice surprise," I tell him when he arrives.

His dark hair hits his shoulders. "I wanted to trim it up before Christmas."

I run a comb through his locks after wrapping a dark blue plastic cape around him. His hair is thick and straight. "How much do you want off?"

A trim to me is a half inch or so. He indicates a much different style. "I'd like to shave the sides and leave it long on top. Sort of spike-y, but not punk rock. Does that make sense?"

People have a variety of descriptions when it comes to a new style and I've discovered the best way to make sure we're on the same page before I take up my scissors is to show them visual ideas.

I grab my phone and present several variations of the modern style he seems to be suggesting. He settles on tapered sides with a low fade and a medium-length, brushed up mohawk.

We chat as I work, and I'm reminded how much I like him and the Redferns. Rain is fun to talk to and easy on the eyes. He's probably the lone guy in town close to my age I haven't dated.

"Your cousin...does she like Christmas?" he asks.

He has a light beard and I groom that, too, matching the length to the sides of his new hairstyle. "Which one?"

I don't really need to clarify this; he made it clear at Thanksgiving he has a crush on Robyn, my cousin who is Story Cove's only detective.

Rain's skin is a lovely tawny color, but I still see a faint tinge of pink on his cheeks when he says, "Detective Woods."

He's too cute. "She grew up in Colorado, and her

parents made a huge deal out of it, so yes, she does. They're gone now, and I know she misses them and the snow. Why do you ask?"

His gaze in the mirror shyly darts away. "I wondered if she was going to the theatre production on Christmas Eve."

"Probably, if she can get away from work."

He toys with the edge of the cape. "She works too much."

I finish his beard. "I agree. I'm sure she'll be at all the events this week, but in an official capacity. If you want to chat with her, you might bring her a coffee or lunch one day."

"I have an extra ticket to the play. Thought I'd invite her to go with me. Maybe we could grab some dinner beforehand."

I like that he's working up the courage to ask her out. Robyn is no easy cookie, but he's so centered and determined, they'd make a good match. "Absolutely. She could use a night of fun, especially on Christmas Eve."

"You think she'll agree to it?"

The look on his face is priceless. He's got it bad, and I better warn Robyn, so *if* she isn't interested, she lets him down gently. "Some risks are worth taking, right?"

He agrees and I see the confidence in his eyes when I'm finished. The new style suits him and he could sweep anyone off their feet at the moment.

He seems to think so as well, thanking me

profusely and tipping liberally. I wish him luck with Robyn and cross my fingers for their potential romance.

Later, I'm cleaning my station, having added another ninety dollars to my bookstore fund and wishing I'd hit my goal of one hundred, when Glenda sticks her head around the corner. "Got a walk-in. Can you take it?"

Maybe my goal is in sight. "Sure. Send her back."

I collect the hair I've swept into a pile and hustle out to dump it. When I return, I stop short.

Sitting in my chair is the last person I want to see.

"Hello, Rebel," Sawyer says to me. "I need help."

"What do you want?"

He eases into my chair. "Your styling expertise."

Right. All he needs is a haircut.

I march to the back room, take several deep breaths, and grab the blue cape that I left to clean after Rain's appointment.

As I shake it out and wipe it down, my pulse races as fast as my mind. Staring mindlessly at the plastic, I play with my hair a moment, winding a long strand around my wrist a couple times. The deep red I summoned this morning starts to brighten, then change.

"No, no, no," I whisper to it. "Not now!"

Sure enough, my magick has a mind of its own again. The rainbow colors start coming fast and furious. Is this reaction caused by Sawyer?

Can't be. The first time it happened, he was nowhere around.

But I was thinking of him, even if it was in order to break the bond between us.

I grab the last of the potion from my purse and drink it down, praying it will stop the kaleidoscope of hues.

"You okay back there?" Sawyer calls.

I curse silently and wind a length of hair around my wrist to calm me. Clearing my throat, I paste on a fake smile to sweeten my voice. "Coming," I respond.

*Here goes nothing.* Focusing on acting nonchalant, I stride to my station and snap the cape around Sawyer's thick neck.

He's big and broad, much more so than Rain. His dark eyes meet mine with steady resolve in the mirror, then follows the shimmering shades running from my roots to the tips of my strands. "That's a new style."

"Festive, isn't it?" I ask, pretending I'm doing it on purpose.

"You look good in anything."

I slide a wide-tooth comb through his thick curls, one of the tines snagging on a knot. He doesn't so much as flinch.

I tug harder, keeping the snicker off my face when he finally winces. "So what are we doing today?" My voice comes out almost normal, neutral. I'm proud of myself.

"Mamaw says I need a trim."

His grandmother sent him. Of course, she did. He didn't come to see me on his own. "How is Minerva?"

He grins. "Sassy as ever."

The comb tangles again. I want to yank it out and scream at him at the same time. What good would it do, though? He left to take care of his mother. I shouldn't fault him for it.

*Be cool*, I tell myself. I tease out the knot. "And your mother?"

He heaves a heavy sigh. "Married again and in South America with the guy."

Sounds par for the course. My curiosity begs for more but I stuff it down. Running my fingers through the long locks at the back of his neck, I force myself to stay detached as can be. "An inch?"

I feel his eyes on me, making my body heat. The corner of his mouth twitches, as if he can tell what that stare does to me. Jerk. "Half."

Normally, I'd offer a shampoo, but the idea of massaging his head makes my belly cramp. A few spritzes from my water bottle is good enough. I grab my scissors and a different comb. "Half it is."

It's been four years since I've touched him. Four years since I've been anywhere near him. He smells of soap and leather. I remember his favorite scent—Devil May Care. A combo of smoke, musk, and whiskey. It was a standard soap for our shop until he broke my heart. Cinder took the inventory we had at that time and threw them out.

My fingers shake ever so slightly as I pull up the

first parted section and raise the scissors. *Look at the bright side, I'll have more of his hair.*

A second batch of potion is possible. That will get me through the coming days and he'll bail after Christmas. *You can handle this.*

"You okay there, Rebel?"

I've paused, scissors hovering in mid-air. He probably thinks I'm deciding whether to trim it or stab him.

Let him wonder. "Never better. I bet Minerva is happy to have you home."

"Thrilled. It's been too long. I never meant to stay away for such a prolonged period. One thing led to the next."

There are plenty more questions I could ask, but my tongue falls mute. It's better if I simply do my job and don't engage in small talk. The only thing I care about when it comes to him can't be resolved with a simple gabfest anyway.

As I cut, he points to the mirror and a photo of my sisters I have secured in the corner. "How's the gang?"

"Fine," I reply tersely. *Clip, clip, clip.*

Strained silence descends. Even the background music is quiet now, Glenda preparing to close for the day. All the other stylists have already left, their booths quiet and clean.

My reticence becomes uncomfortable, and finally he speaks again. "Mamaw says you're remodeling the shop."

"Yes." *Clip, clip, clip.*

"That's awesome. Business must be good."

I wish I was there right now. I need Belle to keep me positive. "We've expanded our product line, and thanks to Cinder's boyfriend and his mother, we've received national exposure."

"If you need any help with the remodel while I'm home—"

"We have plenty, thank you. How long are you in town?"

"Mamaw's having a knee replaced the first of the year. The surgery and follow-up therapy will put her out of commission for a while. She's gonna need help getting around and running her business."

*Clip.* He's staying until she's back on her feet? *Clip.*

"She did so much for me growing up," he continues. "Even though she won't ask for help, I need to be here for her."

That's Sawyer for you, always taking care of the women in his family. It's a good trait, and yet, it drove him from me, so it's difficult to celebrate it.

"Your mother isn't volunteering?"

His demeanor tenses, but he says nothing.

After a few more silent moments, he squirms. "I met Cinder's boyfriend. Nice guy."

I stop mid-comb. Curiosity burns inside me again, but I refuse to ask how he knows Finn. I continue my task. "Yes, he is."

I can tell by the way he tries to hold my gaze in the mirror, even though I won't meet his, that he's frustrated. "Okay, I'd planned to have this conversation later, over dinner maybe, but Zelle, cut me some slack here, will you? I know I screwed up—"

I grab the water bottle and point it at him. "Don't."

He eyes the weapons in my hands. "I deserve your hostility, but I want to make it right."

"Hostility?" My laughter is dry and brittle. I spray his hair, not caring that droplets hit his face. "Why would I feel *anything* for you?"

That hits him deeper than any anger or bitterness I could spew. He wipes a hand over his wet face and reaches for my wrist to fend off another potential shower. "I'm sorry."

*Too little, too late, buddy boy.*

I set the spritz bottle on the counter and resume trimming. I can't speak because I'll break out crying... or maybe I *will* stab him.

He doesn't say anything further, and when I'm done, I brush stray strands from his neck. That spot... *I used to kiss him right there.* My fingers hover over it.

Combined with the smell of his soap and leather vest, a hoard of memories crashes over me, knocking the wind from my lungs and nearly making me bend over.

"Zelle?"

I turn away before he can see the tears burning in my eyes. I pretend I'm brushing off the front of my dress, while I take several deep breaths, focusing on my wedge heels, my painted toenails, the edge of the skirt. It's a trick that Belle taught me when we were little and it helps me control my anxiety.

Anxiety the likes of which I haven't experienced in a long time. Four years, to be exact.

Of course, my hair isn't in on the let's-be-calm program, the strand wrapped around my wrist going wild with vivid colors.

Sawyer comes out of the chair and reaches for me. "You need to sit down. Let me get you some water."

I put out a hand to stop him. "I'm fine. Please go."

"You're not."

I force my gaze to meet his. "Actually, I am, and I'll be even better when you leave."

The pain on his face makes me feel guilty.

*Tough cookies. Apology not accepted.*

Wrinkling the cape as he tugs it off, he shakes his head. "I really am sorry, Rebel."

All I can do is stare at my hair.

"How much do I owe you?" he asks.

"Nothing," I choke out. I ball the material in my hands and walk toward the back room. "Merry Christmas."

# SIX

"He had the audacity to act like things were normal," I tell my family at breakfast the next morning. I pour orange juice for myself and Uncle Odin. "He even asked about 'the gang' and our remodel project."

"Sounds horrible," Matilda says. There's a definite ring of sarcasm. "How dare he be nice to you."

As I give her the evil eye, Cinder tries to hide a snicker.

Belle jumps when I slam the refrigerator door. I place the glass in front of Uncle Odin a touch too hard and juice jumps over the side. Ruby grabs a napkin to wipe it up.

"I don't want nice. There is nothing normal between us and never will be again."

Ruby sets a plate of toast on the table and pats my shoulder. "The eggs are almost ready. Take a breath, sit down, and tell us why your hair keeps changing colors like it is."

I take my seat across from our godmother, who begins buttering a slice. "What do you want from him, Zelle?"

My hair is indeed going through its rainbow effect once more, making me feel a little like Rudolph, lighting up the space around me. I shaved it last night and it's already down past my shoulders this morning.

The first time this occurred, I was bending over the pot breathing in the mist coming from Eunice's potion. After drinking some of the concoction, it continued to happen.

Better to blame the potion than my anxiety over Sawyer.

Everyone is staring at me, waiting for an answer. "I want..." *An apology,* I start to say, but he offered that and it took none of the pain away. It wasn't enough. Not nearly.

I hang my head in my hands. "Closure, I guess. Some peace. But I don't know what he could say or do to give that to me."

Matilda smiles. "That's an inside job, as they say. No one can give you peace. You have to find it yourself."

Belle points at me with a triangle slice. "What about your hair? I mean, it's pretty and all, but maybe you should see a doctor or something. Make sure you're not sick."

"I'm not sure what's causing the color explosion, but I'm not ill."

Cinder has her sketchpad and makes a few tweaks to the drawing she's working on. "At the very least, Sawyer should say he's sorry."

"He already did," I admit.

My sisters exchange a look. Matilda frowns. "He apologized?" She looks skeptical. "Before or after you threatened him with the scissors?"

"It was a spray bottle," I state in my defense, leaving out the fact I considered giving him a haircut he'd never forget.

"Wait, he said he was sorry?" Belle stares at me in confusion, her features tightening. "And you're still upset?"

"He sacrificed our relationship to run after Janice, even after everything she put him and Minerva through all those years. I was there for him every day when she wasn't while we were growing up. I never made him choose me over her, even in high school. But then we were eighteen and ready to start a life together and she ran off, getting herself in trouble yet again. He didn't have to leave—he picked her over me. Sorry doesn't quite cut it."

Cinder accepts the plate of toast and selects a slice. "Sounds like he's trying, though, Zelle. Neither of you can change the past, but maybe you still have a future."

"I know, but..." I slump back in my chair. "I don't know what's wrong with me. I still have this ball of anger inside. All I know is that his apology didn't change anything. I'm still angry."

"That's pain, not anger," Matilda states. "You don't like feeling emotional, so it's easier to morph that into fury. I'm the same way. Did I ever tell you about the troll I dated once?"

"Troll?" Ruby echoes, looking half-afraid and half-intrigued.

Matilda nods enthusiastically. "You want to talk anger issues, he had them. Our fights were legendary."

"He's taking the first step to being friends again," Belle says, switching the conversation back to me and my issues. "Maybe that's how you find closure, sister."

Friends. The word rolls around in my brain like a bowling ball, knocking into the hundreds of memories I have that involve Sawyer.

We met in the principal's office when I was eleven. He was the new kid, waiting for the usual welcome speech and a tour of the school. Slouched in one of two chairs against the wall, his eyes were closed when I walked in, head back as if sleeping. The secretary took the note from my hand and scowled. "Have a seat, Rapunzel. Principal Rolands will be with you soon."

I flinched at hearing my given name, flopping into the other seat and let go of a dramatic sigh. It was a scene she and I had repeated many times in my school career to that point. I gently touched my sore knuckles. There was blood on them from Mallory Denton's nose.

"What are you in for?" Sawyer had asked.

When I glanced at him, I saw him assessing my

hair, as well as my hands. "Pretty obvious, isn't it? Fighting."

That was the first time I saw the lip twitch that doubled as his crooked grin. My heart was never the same.

He retrieved a tissue from the desk. "Did you win?"

I accepted it and dabbed at my scrapes. "Yeah," I claimed confidently. Mrs. Jones looked at me over the top of her glasses. "Sort of," I added. "She called me a freak, which she does regularly, but you don't see her here being punished for bullying kids."

"She's in the nurse's office," Jones stated dryly. "You broke her nose."

"I rearranged the cartilage, but I pulled the punch. It's not broken."

Jones found my response less than amusing.

Rolands threatened to expel me that day, but I think he feared my magickal family, so instead of sending me home, he sentenced me to something worse—he made me stay.

He also assigned me to be Sawyer's tour guide for the day, to make sure he got to all of his classes.

"Who taught you to fight?" he asked as I walked him to the gym for P.E.

"My godmother."

He looked impressed. "Is your name really Rapunzel?"

Was I going to have to punch him, too? "Just Zelle. If you ever call me anything else, I'll rearrange your nose cartilage."

"Okay, Just Zelle." The crooked grin appeared. "But I think Zelle The Rebel has a nice ring to it, don't you?"

The way he said it, complete with a real grin this time, made me pause. I *was* a rebel—more so than any of my sisters. I'd been attempting to live up to all of their standards, and failing miserably at it. Sawyer's grin told me I didn't have to be anything but myself with him.

I don't know what he said to Mallory or her posse, but they never called me "freak" again, no matter what crazy hairdo I came to school with, or what combination of clothes I stole from Matilda's closet and acted like it was fashionable. For a long time, I believed the nose punch was the cure, but I realized later that Sawyer made people nervous, just like I did. When we paired up, no one bullied us.

"Zelle?"

I snap back to the table and breakfast. They're all staring at me again as if they're concerned I've lost it. "Sorry. What did you say?"

Ruby is putting eggs on each person's plate. "You're grooming Ren's rescue dogs for the walk tonight, right?"

I inwardly cringe. I'd forgotten I volunteered to do that. "Don't worry. I'll have those pups looking gorgeous."

This makes Belle smile, and I remember I'm the only one who doesn't enjoy this time of year. The rest of them are quite happy. I give her a signature wink. "We'll find them all a home for Christmas."

My sisters and Uncle Odin dig in, discussing the tree lighting ceremony.

Matilda, however, studies me as she eats. I try to ignore her, since she's attempting to read my mind.

Why anyone would want to jump into that chaos is beyond me.

Finally, she interrupts the others. "I need a space for my Yule ceremony tonight. I'm doing it live on Facebook, too. Thought I'd use the new area of the showroom, like I was going to last month before Ren wolfed out on us."

Ruby scowls. Ren is a shifter who changed into a wolf when several murders occurred before Thanksgiving. "He couldn't help it."

Cinder raises her brows. "What about your usual place?"

Matilda teaches workshops for witchy women developing their inner priestess. At least, that's what she calls it. They do some meditation, play with crystals, and work on spells.

She glances at Belle. "Someone kicked us out."

My twin looks slightly sheepish. "The old fire station is the best spot in town for the gingerbread contest and Meet Santa event."

Matilda rolls her eyes. "Don't worry, Cinder. I'll handle everything, and cleanup is easy."

As she takes her plate over to the sink, I see Cinder's face is, indeed, very worried. I can't blame her. Matilda's events involve burning candles and drinking wine. With her wonky magick, that's a recipe for disaster.

"Don't you want to hold it outside under the moon?" Cinder suggests. "The parking lot has a great view of the sky."

Matilda refills her unicorn travel mug. "Too cold."

She leaves while Cinder stews. I reach over to pat our eldest sister's hand. "After I clean up the dogs, I can come home and keep an eye on her."

"We could put a spell on the room to make it fire-proof," Ruby adds.

"I heard that!" Matilda calls.

"I've got to run," I tell them. I rinse my plate and kiss Ruby's cheek. "Thank you, as always, for the meal."

Before I can escape Enchanted, however, Matilda draws me aside downstairs. "I could pull a few cards, see what the Fates say about you and Sawyer."

Knowing her, she already has. Dabbling in tarot and oracle cards is one of her passions, but she doesn't talk about them much. "There is no *me and Sawyer*," I tell her.

I walk out the door before she can see I'm lying.

# SEVEN

The morning at the salon flies by and so does the afternoon at Enchanted. No one mentions Sawyer to me at either place, and my hair stays the icy blue I chose this morning.

I'm not a groomer, but Ruby and Ren are hard to say no to. When Ren asked a few days ago if I'd clean up the rescues he took in and trim their coats for the downtown walk, I agreed.

He threw in a free check-up for Rumpelstiltskin, and agreeing to help him pleased Ruby, so it was worth it. Keeping my sisters happy has been my goal ever since our parents died.

When late afternoon rolls around, Ruby and I head to the clinic. She bathes each dog before passing them to me. There's a chihuahua-terrier mix, a schnauzer, a poodle, and another puppy we call Heinz 57 because none of us have a clue what genes he's made of.

Ren rounds things out by clipping their nails, and

within an hour, we have four pristine fur balls ready to put in the window of the clinic to show them off. I add a bow to the poodle who Ren named Miss Lady, and the schnauzer, Gladius, looks quite distinguished with the beard I left around his muzzle.

Ren's parrot, George, and Ruby's raven, Lenore, cackle and talk the whole time. I enjoy Ruby's laughter at Ren's gentle teasing. They make a good pair. Even their birds get along.

As I'm packing up my scissors and combs, Ruby hugs and thanks me. "See you at six for the tree lighting."

Like most of the town, I look forward to the ceremony and seeing my angel on the Wishing Tree. Every year, I've tied a ribbon on the branches, and many have come true. My sisters are happy, Nonni and Poppi are healthy, Uncle Odin and Matilda continue to live with us, even though we're grown and no longer need supervision.

Outside of everyone's health and happiness, I don't have a wish for this year.

I think about staying in my room to listen to Elvis, drink hot cocoa, and play with my hair. Maybe I can figure out why it keeps doing what it's doing.

Enchanted is packed with shoppers when I return, so I pitch in to help with the rush. After closing, I restock shelves while Cinder pours Christmas Hearth candles. As soon as I'm done, I sneak upstairs, ready to enact my plan.

Belle knows me too well, however. "Why aren't

you ready?" She looks horrified to see me in my flannel pajamas. "Don't think for a minute you're bailing on me."

"You have plenty of support. You don't need me."

She eases down on the edge of the bed next to my leg. "I always need you,. This is a big deal for me—being chairwoman of the Christmas event. I want you there."

Matilda strolls by regaled in a bright fuchsia top and yellow skirt. Pom poms swing wildly from the hem. "She's just scared."

I glare at her, even though I can't see her as she continues down the hall. "I am not," I call.

She reappears in the doorway, leaning against the jamb. "Guess you'll have to come to the Yule ceremony downstairs. The women will love you." She crosses the floor to tug on one of my braids. "They'll want to play with your hair."

Our godmother likes to fight dirty. "No one touches it, and for your information, I'm not scared of anything."

"Prove it." She walks to the exit and looks at me over her shoulder. "Go to the lighting. Who cares if Sawyer's there?"

I feel like a petulant child. "I'm not staying in because of him."

"Aren't you?" Belle asks.

I can see in their faces they think I'm acting like a heartbroken teenager, rather than a strong, independent and confident witch.

Maybe I do still need adult supervision, or at least a kick in the pants from time to time.

Reluctantly, I admit my shortcomings. "I'm sorry for the way I've been acting. My heart is more raw than I expected it to be from seeing him again."

Matilda smiles. "That's life, kid. Take that pain and do what us Valkyries do."

Matilda often refers to the fact she was a warrior in some far off lifetime. Maybe that's where her magick comes from. None of us are sure.

"What is that, exactly?"

She makes a fist and shakes it. "Turn it into courage, determination, and fight, like I taught you."

I once again remember Mallory and her nose. I was a rebel then, and I still am. Nothing, not even a broken heart, is going to keep me from that lighting.

When she disappears down the steps, Belle pats my hand. "I'd be more scared of her and her witches descending on you than running into Sawyer."

I push off the bed and head for my closet. "I am."

Fifteen minutes later, I'm among the crowd in front of City Hall. The street is roped off, and a large crowd of people are talking and laughing. The weather is chilly enough some folks wear scarves and mittens. I've chosen a wool jacket, knee-high boots, and finger-less gloves.

Uncle Odin stands next to me, pointing out certain ornaments he likes. Finn and Cinder are on their way, while Ruby and Ren are at the clinic, hoping to adopt out the dogs.

Belle rushes past to supervise a city worker using a boom lift to add the angel to the top of the wishing tree. A golden star is perched on the peak of the other, both a sight to behold.

I force myself not to scan the gathering, speaking to many folks as they mill around, and watching some write out their wishes on a nearby table. The top is covered with ribbons, just waiting for them.

Kids run up and down the steps of City Hall, others work on their wishes. There are plenty of folks in town and the surrounding area who've had it hard this year, like Belle said last week. One of the nearby factories closed its doors, and the economy has been up and down like a rollercoaster. We've been lucky at Enchanted that none of that has affected us.

Robyn is making the rounds, and I see Rain approach her. I've been so caught up in my own issues, I forgot to warn her about his potential invite.

When I see a rare smile cross her face at the sight of him, I relax. The guy might do just fine on his own.

Sawyer and Minerva cut through the throng. They each carry cups of steaming cider, and she offers her extra to Uncle Odin.

"Yes, excellent," he says, accepting one. "Snow's cider is perfect for tonight, don't you think? The kids love watching her use her press to make it fresh."

Sawyer extends one of his to me. "Here you go."

I wave him off. "No thanks, I'm good."

Minerva's wrinkles are deep, but she's not that old. Sometimes a hard life can do that to you, especially when you worry over family. "Thank you for trimming Sawyer's hair without an appointment." Her eyes gleam in the lights from the tree. "You're always so kind, Zelle. Just like your mother."

That's debatable, but I offer a gracious smile. "It was no trouble."

"I've never known you to turn down apple cider, my dear," Uncle Odin says to me. His tone is light and breezy, as always, but I catch the underlying chastisement in it.

"It's just a drink," Sawyer murmurs, continuing to extend the cup, "not a declaration of forgiveness if you accept it. You can drink it and go right on hating me."

A cheer goes up as the angel is secured and the lift descends. Belle is delighted, her cheeks flushed. She grins at me with achievement shining on her face.

A couple adjacent to Uncle Odin engage him and Minerva in conversation about the evening's festivities. Against my better judgment, I take the cider from Sawyer. "I don't hate you."

He rocks back slightly, watching the activity. "Well, I still appreciate the fact you didn't stab me yesterday."

Matilda would have a snappy comeback. I search for one, but before I can come up with it, Belle takes to the platform at the top of the steps, quieting the crowd. The children chasing each other race to their parents. "Welcome everyone to Christmas in Story Cove!"

The gathered crowd cheers. Since one hand is full, I can't clap, but I whistle.

My twin meets my eyes, notices Sawyer next to me, and gives a thumbs-up. The group believes it's for them; I know it's directed at me.

She recites the itinerary for this night, and the next four leading up to the big day. She's packed the schedule full. Along with the tree lighting and downtown walk, there's the quilt show, the rescue dogs for adoption, Snow has a petting zoo in the park, run by her boyfriend and farmhand Broden, and there are sleigh rides. We even have a cart selling roasted chestnuts and popcorn, and local crafters have their wares for sale inside the former fire station, along main avenue, and in the park as well. Plenty wait for this event to do all of their shopping in one fell swoop.

"Now, let's get to it." Belle's voice is filled with joy. "Let's light some trees!"

Again there's a roar from those gathered, followed by exuberant clapping. Once she quiets them down, she introduces the two children chosen from dozens of entrants who get to flip the switches. They've been selected by the council as the Christmas in Story Cove ambassadors.

Cody Watson, a young boy in a wheelchair, waves when introduced. Each year he makes dozens of origami gifts for kids in hospitals, and participates in the Special Olympics. He's paralyzed from the waist down, but his positive energy is infectious, and his parents beam with pride.

The other is a girl named Shelby Larins, who's fighting cancer. The six-year-old is wearing a wig made from hair I've donated to the Locks for Love organization. I recognize the silver and white strands, and am grateful someone benefits from my out-of-control mane.

Shelby's brother holds her hand and helps her up the ramp to the giant red switch. Her mother, Megan, a harried woman, watches with tears in her eyes.

Belle leads the countdown, the crowd joining in. "Three...two..."

Sawyer nudges me. I add my voice to the rest. "One!"

Both kids flip their respective switches and the trees come to life. The spectators cheer and I leave Sawyer, making my way to Megan. I know she doesn't have extra money any time of the year, especially not Christmas.

I hand her a business card. "When you have time, call me and schedule an appointment," I tell her. "It's on the house. We can do your hair, a manicure, whatever you want."

She thanks me profusely and I slip off, looking at the stars as I walk home.

Matilda and her witches are wrapping up their Yule celebration, and my godmother is in good spirits. Several of the women made her gifts and this pleases her. We clean up the area in no time, and she retires to take a bubble bath.

A few hours later, my sisters arrive. Ruby's ecstatic

—all four dogs are going to good homes. After the tree lighting, Cinder, Finn, and Leo, Belle's boyfriend, walked around downtown, enjoying the night. Along the way, they met up with Snow and Broden.

They stop in, too, everyone in good spirits. We share some of Ruby's candies around the kitchen table. Belle arrives, grinning from ear to ear, her event kicked off successfully.

Even though I'm tired, I sit at the table with all of them, Uncle Odin joining us. Cinder is relieved Matilda didn't burn down the shop.

I'm listening to the others talk, content that I at least saw the angel tree lighting and remembering the feel of my mother's hand in mine when we went as a family all those years ago. I miss her and Dad every day.

The landline on the wall rings and Belle gets up to answer. "Hello?"

Her face contorts as she listens, and mine tightens in response. "Oh no. How could that happen?" she queries the caller.

"What is it?" I come to my feet. I fear it could be something with Nonni and Poppi.

The others fall silent and Belle holds up a finger to me. "Okay, well thanks for letting me know. I can't believe it, but I'll find another topper. We won't let this ruin our event!"

She hangs up and faces us. "That was Robyn. She was just leaving the station and noticed something was wrong with the wishing tree."

My stomach drops from the sadness on my twin's face. "What is it?"

She meets my eyes and I realize she hates what she has to tell me.

"Belle, what is it?" I demand. "What happened?"

She bites her bottom lip. "The angel topper is gone. Someone has stolen it."

CHAPTER

# EIGHT

Ruby is an early riser. Me? Not so much. After fighting another night of insomnia, I'd do anything to sleep. She catches me in her new kitchen around four a.m. while I'm experimenting with potions. Again.

She brings me coffee which is my usual drink of choice, while she stirs hot cocoa with a candy cane. "What are you brewing up now?"

"It's a...surprise," I say, slipping the recipe under a towel.

She climbs up on a stool and sniffs the air. "Hmm. Rosehips, sweet almond oil... It certainly smells intoxicating. Love potion?"

I snort. "Hardly. You'll find out Christmas morning."

Her face lights up with anticipation. "Are you creating a new line of—"

"No guessing!"

She sips her drink and mulls this over. "I'm sorry about the angel."

"Me, too." Leaning on the counter, I savor the smell of the coffee and test how hot the liquid is. Just right. "Who would steal it, and why?"

"Belle is beside herself. She is taking this very personally."

"It's not her fault." Even as I say it, I know my twin believes it, though.

"True, but the angel has a special tie to you, that makes her overly protective of it."

While I'm upset it's missing, I don't want Belle stressing over it because of me. "It's not valuable from a monetary standpoint and anyone who tried to sell it would be a fool. People from miles around know that's the Story Cove angel. The wishing tree gets a write up every year in all the local papers and on social media."

Ruby fiddles with a jar of scent left on the work table, then eyes the two rows of fresh product. The Yule & Fig candles Cinder made before bed are curing and need to be labeled.

She goes to the new filing cabinet and withdraws a sheet of stickers. "It's a powerful symbol for many. Maybe someone is hoping for their own personal miracle."

The town is full of folks that could apply to. "Half the folks here could use a miracle in one way or another. The culprit should have put his or her wish on the tree like everyone else."

Ruby nods, peeling off stickers and labeling the tins. "No wish for you this year?"

Of course, she would notice. "Since I have the same one I always do, there's no point. I would need some honest to goodness magick mojo to see that come true."

I busy myself cleaning up the ingredients, and hide the samples I've made. Since my sisters believe I'm making haircare products, and I would like to develop a line of them, why not? I've made enough of Eunice's heal-a-broken-heart potion to last me a lifetime, and I'm not sure it's actually helping. As long as I can't sleep, I might as well toy with something that could help women have a good hair day every day, and make a little pocket money as well.

"Mom and Dad are always with us in our hearts," she says.

I wonder if that's why my anxiety is so high again —I'm trying to hold space for all those I've loved and lost, and my heart is stuffed to the max.

I ignore her sad smile, my heart pinching. Tears well in my eyes, so I reach for the anger I've held onto all these years to bat it away. Matilda's right; it's easier to tap into that than deal with sorrow.

Trouble is...this morning, the fire I usually find is only a tiny spark.

Discreetly, I use the towel to dab at the stupid water leaking from my eyes, and end up wrapped in Ruby's arms. I can't hold back any longer and suddenly the dam breaks. I sob on my sister's shoulder, the ugly cry champion of the world.

"Life has been harder on you than any of us," she soothes, rubbing my back. "You've always hidden your deep emotional reserves from the world, but I know how wounded you are."

"I'm not." It's a lie, and sounds ridiculous when I hiccup a sob while saying it. I wipe my nose. "I'm tough like Matilda."

"You *are*, but it's to cover your sensitivity. Ever since you started school and the other kids made fun of your tresses, you armored up. Your hair, your emotions, everything. And you form such intense bonds with those you love, it rips your heart out when they leave."

I cling to her robe. From the corner of my eye, I see my locks going through their colorful display. Definitely tied to my emotions. "I can't stand it. It hurts too much."

Ruby strokes my head. "I know, but it's okay for you to admit you're angry and grieving. You don't have to keep it all bottled up. We're here for you, Z. That's what sisters are for."

The crying jag lasts for another minute or so. The hiccups grow more intense. Ruby makes a special tea and forces me to drink it. It tastes like grass, but it stops my affliction and I'm grateful for that.

For her, too.

Once I'm semi-normal, I pressure her to promise not to tell the others about my breakdown. Belle has too much on her plate right now, and Cinder doesn't need to worry about me more than she already does. Reluctantly, Ruby agrees.

I fall asleep, the emotional flood releasing pent up energy I couldn't get rid of previously. The dreamless sleep carries me until my alarm goes off a few hours later. At first, I feel hung over, but after a shower, my hair is calm and so am I.

I leave it straight and trim it so it hangs just below my ears, its natural silver and white strands framing my face. My eyes are puffy but a bit of concealer and some bright lipstick work to diminish the effect.

"You look bright-eyed and all that," Matilda says at breakfast.

Ruby has made waffles this morning and I accept one with a giant mug of coffee, after feeding the ferret. "I'm going to find a new angel for the tree," I announce.

Belle smiles at me from across the table. "I may have a lead on one. I'll let you know." She hands me my favorite apple syrup.

I drown my food in the gooey stuff. "Excellent."

"Your hair looks nice," Matilda says, digging into her own. "We haven't seen it that natural in years."

Ruby winks at me and I keep eating. "Sometimes natural is best."

Come opening time, I help in the shop. Rainhart stops in.

"She said yes," he gushes. His hair has been styled perfectly, just like I showed him. "We're attending the theatre production together. She can't go for dinner beforehand, but she said she'd like a raincheck."

"I'm happy for you." I wink at him. "She's a great person. Just be sure you treat her right, or I'll have to come after you, okay?"

His smile falters as he tries to decide if I'm joking or not.

Matilda swings by on her way to the cash register. "She has a mean right hook. You've been warned."

Rain chuckles. "I heard you were tough."

He has no idea. "Runs in the family. Robyn can take care of herself, and I'm kidding about coming after you. Sort of."

I smile, but it does nothing to convince him I'm teasing. "Well, I, uh... Thanks for the encouragement. I promise to treat her like a princess? A queen?"

"She's not really a fairytale type of gal. Just be sure you're kind, considerate, and funny. She prefers guys with a sense of humor."

He points a finger at me. "Got it. I was thinking I'd give her a little something for Christmas. Perhaps a candle. Does she like those?"

"I have her favorite stashed in the back." It's a popular one for fall, but we had to make room for the Christmas products. "She also enjoys our lime soap."

When I return with the Autumn Breeze candle, Matilda is bagging several bars of Luscious Lime for Rain. "I think I'll give it a try, too," he tells me, sniffing at one. "Smells great."

"She rides her bike in the National Park," I offer as I

add the candle to his purchases. "Even in the winter. If you enjoy brisk tours through the woods, you might suggest one after the holidays."

He's so excited, he's nearly vibrating. He pays and thanks us before leaving.

"Did you set that up?" my godmother asks.

"Nope, he instigated it all on his own."

"I can't believe Robyn agreed to a date." Matilda fiddles with her red and white Santa earrings. "She likes being on her own."

"Tis the season for miracles," I chirp.

She narrows her eyes at me. "Seems so."

That afternoon, I meet with the main cast members of the theatre production. Their moderately extended version of the classic holiday story doesn't call for much in the way of hairstyles, but the makeup will need to be bold and easy to see from the audience.

Mrs. Winthrop, who is a regular client with flamboyant tastes, insists I accompany her to the amphitheater to get 'a feel' for the troop's needs. Since she allowed me to give her my most favorite hairstyle — the snowy slopes cut and color that brought three more ladies in for the same last week, I owe her.

The small outdoor stage is on the far edge of town. Everyone's breath frosts in the air.

Finn is there with his mother, Mrs. Starling, who's calling out cues and prompting actors with their lines. She was a famous eighties film star and is a huge financial benefactor. While she is a bit over the top with everything, she's actually great at infusing life into this group and their performances. She's brought good publicity to the town, and the theater is not the only group benefiting from her presence. My sisters and I are very grateful for her support of our products.

Which reminds me of the last minute orders I need to mail. I set a reminder on my phone to take them to the post office and overnight them so that they arrive in time for Christmas.

"Hey, Zelle," a familiar voice calls.

My happy mood souring, I look up to see Sawyer with a paintbrush in hand on stage. He smiles. "Nice day, isn't it?"

He's staining a section of the floor that's been repaired. Finn is on his knees, doing the same.

The sun is blinding as I peer up at the two of them, the hulking back hood of the stage echoing the acoustics of the actors running through their lines.

Mrs. Winthrop glances at me, waiting for a response. I can't find my voice. It's lost somewhere in my chest at the sight of Sawyer in a cut-off t-shirt that displays his massive biceps. One sports an artistic heart, with fancy scrollwork.

I feel the world closing in around me as I read the single word written through it.

*Rebel.*

Realizing I'm speechless, Mrs. Winthrop smiles at both men. "It's gorgeous. Perfect December weather." She grabs my arm and tugs. "We'll let you get back to work. Lots to do before Christmas Eve!"

Numbly, I follow her to the rear of the theatre,

climbing the steps and only half-listening as she walks me to the area set aside for costume changes and such. "Will this do?" she asks

"What? Oh, sure." There are several tables with mirrors. I set one up for hair and a second for makeup. "What time can I get started?"

"As early as you want. Santa will require the most work, don't you think? But since it's your uncle playing the part, you can fix him up at home, I suppose."

Right. Uncle Odin is playing Santa not just in the performance, but also for the kids during the event tonight at the old fire station. I have to get him ready.

We finish figuring out the details and she offers to drop off the stage makeup she has in stock from the last several productions. I thank her and head back to Main Street.

As I'm walking away, Finn calls goodbye. I wave over my shoulder without glancing back.

Rebel. Zelle, my rebel.

I swallow the confusing emotions Sawyer's tattoo has generated, making a beeline for Enchanted and my to-do list.

In the back room at the shop, Rumpelstiltskin is delighted to see me and jumps into my arms. I hug him tight and whisper, "You're the best familiar ever. Just don't tell Jayne."

He snuggles under my chin and chitters as though he understands. I know he does.

Robyn is here. "Hi, Zelle."

I wave. "What's that?"

She's holding her phone and showing Cinder something. "A video from the security cameras posted on City Hall that recorded our thief."

She taps the screen to zoom in as I look over my sister's shoulder. Rumpel leans in as well, as if studying the recording, too.

The black and white footage is grainy. "Can't tell much about our perpetrator," Robyn says. "The tree is at least ten feet tall, the boom lift is approximately six in the air. From the shape and size of our culprit, I'm guessing it's a woman, approximately five foot three, maybe a few inches taller."

The ferret squirms, already bored, and I set him down. He scampers off to the tower stairs to cause havoc up there. Shrugging off my jacket, I watch as the person reaches out a gloved hand from their position behind the tree, stretching up and over to snag the angel. Dressed in dark colors, a hood hiding their head, there are no identifying elements visible.

"It's as if the thief knew about the cameras," Cinder comments.

Robyn nods in agreement. "She keeps her face turned from this one as she climbs down once the angel is in hand."

We continue to watch until the culprit disappears.

"What can we do to help you catch her?" Cinder asks.

Robyn puts her cell away. "With so little to go on, I'm not sure we'll be able to solve this anytime soon. Keep your eyes open and your ears peeled, will you?"

She's looking at me. I hear so much gossip, you never know what I might come across. "Of course. No one wants to get it back more than I do. I don't want Belle stressing over this."

"I know she's upset," Robyn says, "but I'll stay on this. In the meantime, we need to find an alternate topper."

"Where *is* Belle?" I ask Cinder.

Out front in the shop, I hear someone enter and Ruby calls a greeting. "Hi, Leo. How are you today?"

"At the bookstore." Cinder piles packages together as Leo answers Ruby. "She has to get the station prepped for tonight."

"I'll run those to the post office after I get some coffee." I tell her, pointing at the parcels.

"I gotta run," Robyn says. "See you guys tonight."

Leo enters, nodding to Robyn as she passes by. He holds out a key to me. "Here you go. The unit is number SC212 located on the west end."

I look at him dumbfounded, craning my neck to meet his eyes. "What are you talking about."

"Didn't you get Belle's message?"

I check my phone and find a request for me to search Leo's storage unit where he keeps boxes of antique Christmas items. My twin hopes I can find a replacement angel. "Ah, okay." I accept the key. How am I going to fit this into my day on top of everything else?

"I'd do it," Leo tell me, "but I have an out-of-town client to meet today and because of the holiday, we can't postpone it." He hands me a folded paper, part diagram, part spreadsheet. "Boxes 1173, 1601, and 1944 are your best bets to find a replacement."

I see the box numbers highlighted on the spreadsheet. "No problem."

"I must warn you—while the unit is organized by decades, and color coded as to type of holiday decorations, it's packed floor to ceiling. The boxes are heavy. You'll need help."

Great. The doorbell jingles, and I hear Ruby greet a new customer.

"Is Matilda around?" I question Cinder. I really need to talk to my older sister about Sawyer and the tattoo, but there's not time right now.

"What do you need help with, dear?"

I turn to find Uncle Odin standing behind me.

"Moving boxes," I tell him.

I assume he's about to volunteer, when he says, "I'm sure young Sawyer could assist you."

As soon as he moves fully into the room, Sawyer is revealed behind him.

"Hi," he says. "You ran away before we could talk."

Rumpelstiltskin barrels in once more and dances on his back feet to claw at Sawyer's leg.

"Talk?" I step back. "About what?"

Sawyer bends down and pets Rumpel's head. Uncle Odin holds up a garment bag. "Sawyer helped me locate the Santa outfit for tonight. I dare say, it could use a dry cleaning, but no time for that, is there? Maybe one of those potions you have could freshen it a bit?"

Cinder takes the bag from him. "I'll hang it outside to air out. You two go look for the angel."

Traitor. "But..."

Leo nods at Sawyer. "Hey, good to see you again." They exchange a manly handshake.

"You two know each other?" I ask.

"Yeah," Leo answers. "Sawyer is doing some work for me at the mansion after Christmas. Finn recommended him. I've got bedrooms I want to fix up." He points at the paper I'm holding. "There's a lot to sort through. You better get started. Gotta run!"

He practically runs out, and I smell a rat. What are he and Belle up to?

"Why is he working on bedrooms?" I ask, more to Cinder than Sawyer.

My sister shrugs with a grin on her face. "I don't know, maybe he's anticipating having a family one of these days."

Ah. Right. Belle is keen on having children, and the idea of becoming an aunt makes me smile.

Cinder directs Uncle Odin to go, the Santa outfit in hand. "Don't forget those packages," she calls over her shoulder.

Sawyer gathers them as I reluctantly put on my jacket. "I don't need help," I insist.

"You never did."

He stands there, packages in hand, waiting.

Rumpel wants to go and I figure it will be good for him. I stuff him in my jacket. "You can just put those in the van and be on your way."

He trails after me to the rear parking lot and dutifully places them inside the vehicle. He then climbs into the passenger seat.

I glare at him as I start the engine. "I said I don't need help."

He stares straight ahead. "How about some company?"

Breathing slowly in and out of my mouth, I stare at

my hands on the steering wheel. My nail polish is chipped and I mentally scan through my list of favorite polishes in my head, controlling my rapid pulse. I don't need to look in the mirror, to know my hair is going crazy with colors. "I *have* company."

On cue, the ferret sticks his head from my jacket.

Sawyer reaches over and scratches his head. "Look, I know you're mad as a hornet's nest, but I need to stay away from the quilt shop. Far away. You'd be doing me a real favor if you take me with you. Whatever punishment you want to dish out, I accept. I won't even talk to you if that's what you want."

"Why are you avoiding your grandmother's shop?"

"It's quilting club day. She has the monthly meeting this morning, then she's having an open house this afternoon so folks can come and vote on the Christmas quilts."

"Afraid the club ladies will try to show you how to quilt?"

He makes a face. "Worse. They're all trying to marry me off to their daughters and granddaughters."

Irritation and jealousy war inside my chest. The two of us stare at each other for a long moment, his dark eyes glinting with mischief.

Resolve crumbling, the rebel inside goads me on. I put the van in gear and take off.

CHAPTER

# TEN

After mailing the packages, we find the storage unit is exactly as Leo described. Shelving lines the walls and several run down the center, forming aisles. Every square inch houses containers, stacked and packed, numbered and color-coordinated.

Rumpelstiltskin takes off, curious at all the enticing boxes. In one corner devoid of shelves, vintage Christmas trees stand like a small forest. Some are metal. One is colored pink, another blue. The life-like versions are sprinkled with fake snow. Victorian Santas stare at us as Sawyer and I stand and take it all in.

He whistles under his breath. "Impressive."

It is that. "Ruby would appreciate this level of organization. She can't even get me to arrange my makeup shelf at home."

"You take that side." Sawyer points to the left. "I'll do this."

The overhead lighting isn't very bright and I squint at the cartons high above my head on the top shelf. I take out my phone and use my flashlight app, counting off the numbers. "Box 1601 should be over here," I tell him.

"I'm searching for 1173."

We each scan our respective stacks. "Who do you think stole the angel?" Sawyer asks.

Rumpel peeks from around a carton filled with ornaments, startling me, and I nearly drop my cell. "No idea. Robyn thinks it's a woman."

"Finn's hiring a private investigator to search for it."

I doubt Robyn will appreciate that. I move the ferret out of the way. "You and Finn buddies now, too?"

"He and Leo are good guys. I'm looking forward to Leo's remodel project. I mean, since I'm going to be in town for a while, I might as well work."

"You sure made friends with them fast."

He scans a line of containers on the bottom of his section. "I met Finn in Atlanta several years ago. Did some design work for two craftsman houses for one of his builder clients. He recommended me to Leo. Nothing more than that."

Sawyer always had a way with his hands. "Still doing custom woodwork?"

"It's my bread and butter. In Atlanta, I had this

fantastic shop, all laid out just the way I wanted it, a waiting list of clients..."

His voice fades and I turn to face him, putting Rumpel back on the floor. "What happened?"

He stares at a box of snow globes, brow furrowed. "A business investment group bought up the whole area. The city council re-zoned the place, forcing me and a dozen others out."

I watch my familiar try to climb a pine tree, and grab him off a lower branch. Fake snow comes with him, dusting his tiny paws. "I'm so sorry."

He blinks and shakes off the memory. "Nah, it's all right. It made me reevaluate my life. I realized how much I missed this town. My grandmother may not have many years left, and I don't want to waste them." He glances over at me. "It made me realize how much I miss you."

Before the tsunami of emotions can hit, I whirl away, setting Rumpelstiltskin on the ground. "How's Rena?"

His mother, a wild soul with no love of responsibility, was the reason he left in the first place.

"On her fourth husband. Last I heard from her, she's living off the grid in the Yucatán."

"You're kidding."

"Swear on Mamaw's bible." He pulls a dusty box from the shelf. "Here it is, 1173."

I move over to the large, heavy container and kneel as he places it on the concrete floor. Lifting the lid, the smell of dried cardboard from long ago Christmases, and the tang of old metal, hit my nose.

Consulting the spreadsheet, I note the color and the corresponding decade. A chill from the cool ground seeps into my legs. "This group of items is from the early nineteen-hundreds."

The ferret places his front paws on the edge, peering over and into the box, no doubt sizing up what to him looks like new playthings. Sawyer, on the other side, lifts several oversized silver ornaments off the top. "What a collection."

Layer by layer, we uncover vintage Santas, snowmen, and porcelain trees. The trees have tiny colored lights on the end of their branches that light up when plugged in. Everything is well packed and we're careful to not unwrap anything we don't need, but I'm curious. Like Rumpel-stiltskin, I find it fascinating and I want to check it all out.

The ferret sniffs and paws at some of the items as I remove them. His minute paws dig at the packing paper and bubble wrap. Several times, I have to redirect his attention so he doesn't wreck anything.

A set of postcards with winter scenes and messages in elaborate script catches my attention. I'd love to take the time to read them. Belle found a pack of our grandparents' love letters last month, and we've all enjoyed getting a peek at their lives back in the early 1800s. For a brief moment, I wonder if any of these might have been from them.

As we near the bottom, a tree topper emerges. Not

an angel, but a glass star, wrapped carefully in modern-day bubble wrap.

"Will this do?" Sawyer holds it up, the white glass iridescent under the lights.

Its beauty is unquestionable, but I know Belle—and the rest of the town—will want an angel. "Put it aside, and we'll keep it as a backup, but let's keep looking."

An hour later, we have two. Both are enchanting, their faces serene and their wings unfurled. I have a feeling I know which Belle will pick, but either will work. I'm just relieved we actually found potential replacements and my twin can rest easy about the wishing tree's mascot.

We also found a vintage Santa I fell in love with. Not quite the same as an angel, and probably won't make the cut, but he looks a lot like Uncle Odin, and Santa does grant wishes. Reluctantly, I repack the star topper, knowing I can't have them all.

I place Santa in the van with the angels, as Sawyer locks up the storage unit. The sky is overcast and the breeze brisk. Rumpel cuddles inside my jacket. It almost feels like it could snow.

On the way back to town, Sawyer adjusts the heat and pets the ferret when he leaves my lap. Rumpel happily nestles in his. "Do kids still bring letters to the shop for Santa?"

Because Uncle Odin has white hair and a beard, children often mistake him for the jolly old elf. "We get a few. They honestly believe Santa lives in their home town all year round."

"I always secretly hoped he was," Sawyer confesses. "I mean, it makes sense. You guys are magickal and so is he. I figured you and your sisters might be elves, and you moved to Georgia under a witness protection program or something."

This makes me laugh. I remember his mother could never be bothered with Christmas, so the only dose of it he received was when he hung out with me at the shop. My mom always made sure he had a gift under the tree, in case there were none at home.

"Do you still donate your hair to that wig group?"

Since it grows at such an astronomical rate and I shave it every day, it only makes sense to find a use for it. "Every month I give a bag to Locks for Love."

"I thought so, it looked like your hair on that little girl last night. She's had it rough, huh?"

My pet returns to my jacket. His warm body feels right in my lap. "She has a type of lymphoma and her mom's alone. No insurance, from what I understand, and the hospital bills and medications have nearly bankrupted them. Shelby's aunt started a GoFundMe page and a few of the local organizations have held raffles and other fundraisers, but I'm sure it's still hard to make ends meet."

"That stinks. And the boy in the wheelchair?"

"Some kind of muscle disease. His family is trying to raise money to build a ramp. A few of the locals made one a year ago, but a spring storm tore up the southwest corner of their house, uprooting one of the foundation supports. Folks have been donating time and money to get it fixed, but progress is slow since it affected the foundation. Everything has to be done by professionals and meet housing codes on that before the ramp can be replaced."

"I'd like to help if I can."

I give the ferret one of his treats, and he eats happily away at it as we pass Nonni and Poppi's farm. "I'm sure the Watsons would appreciate it."

Sawyer points at the gate. "How are your grandparents?"

"They're doing well. Nonni's excited about the quilt contest. She's been hard at work for months on her entry. She won't show it to me, but I suspect it's an angel."

Snow and Broden, next door, are out chopping wood. I wave as we pass, and they return it. I see how Snow narrows her eyes at my passenger and continues to watch the van as we drive out of sight. I think about how happy my sisters and cousin are this year, owing to the fact they've all fallen in love.

At the shop, Belle meets us before we can get our coats off. "Well? Did you find one?"

Ruby rushes in to see as well, rubbing her hands together. "Don't keep us in suspense!"

Rumpel takes off the minute I set him down. Sawyer places the items on the back room work table. "They're all excellent replacements," he tells my sisters. "Zelle did good."

"I had help," I remind him.

He winks at me, removes his coat, and assists me in unwrapping our finds.

Belle watches, her eyes lit with anticipation. "I knew I could count on you," she says to me.

I know my twin better than anyone and I'm sure she'll prefer the shimmering white and silver angel over the one dressed in green velvet, but we present both, along with the Santa, and then stand back for her decree.

"So pretty," Ruby says running her finger over each angel.

Belle immediately takes Santa out of the running. She scrutinizes the angels, but it only takes seconds for her to declare the white and silver one the winner. She lifts it up, as if imagining how it will look on top of the tree. "It's not your angel, Zelle, but it will do."

"The original is not *mine*, either," I remind her. "It belongs to the town."

"And we're going to find it." Sawyer reassures her, although he's staring at me.

"I like the Santa." Ruby admires him, stroking his white beard. "Is he a topper, too?"

I smile. "He resembles Uncle Odin, don't you think? I was hoping Leo might sell him to me. I'd like to put him on our tree."

My sisters agree that it's a close replica of our beloved uncle. "Speaking of Santa and uncle Odin," Belle says, "shouldn't you be getting him ready for tonight?"

I check the time and gasp. "Can you put the angel on the tree by yourself?"

"I'll handle it," Sawyer tells us. He begins wrapping the victor back up. "You guys do what you need to do."

"Thank you." Belle kisses his cheek. "Be sure to secure it so no one can steal this one."

"Santa himself won't be able to get it off once I'm done with it."

She and Ruby leave, chatting about the upcoming evening. I walk Sawyer to the door, the angel secured under his arm. "Thank you."

He touches my hand, just a whisper of his fingers. "We *will* find it, Zelle. You can stop acting like it doesn't bother you that it's missing. You should make a wish and put it on the tree."

"How do you know I didn't?"

He gives me that lazy smile that makes me think he knows everything about me. "It's the season of miracles. I know no one, not even the angels or Santa Claus, can bring your parents back, maybe they're wishing you'd find some peace this time of year. That can come from simply remembering how much they loved you."

He's gone before I can reply.

# CHAPTER
# ELEVEN

Bing Crosby belts out a jolly tune from the overhead speakers as Uncle Odin and I hide in the former locker room of the old fire station and wait for his grand appearance.

The place doesn't look much different than it did before the county built a new, improved building several miles north. The big bay doors and concrete walls now offer the town a community gathering spot. With the attached kitchen, folks even rent it out for family reunions, bar mitzvahs, and wedding receptions.

Tonight, it's decorated with holiday cheer. Uncle Odin is definitely the best Santa I've ever seen, wearing the costume with perfect aplomb. Using my enchanted brushes, I've carefully brightened his cheeks with a smidge of blush to make him seem as though he's been out in the cold, and I stuffed his belly with a pillow.

"Suck it in," I tell him as I tighten his wide, black belt one extra notch to make sure it doesn't shift when kids sit on his lap.

He laughs and hums along with the crooner, enjoying the idea of making the children happy.

Matilda shows up dressed in a Mrs. Claus suit that shows off her generous assets. "I'm here, I'm here!" She's out of breath. "Glad you didn't start without me."

"Where did you find that costume?" I ask, fearing it may be a bit risqué for a kids' event. "The Halloween store?"

She glances down at her legs, black nylons, and over the knee boots, displaying several inches of thigh under a short skirt. "It's a bit small, isn't it?"

Skin-tight is more like it. Belle is going to croak.

Her generously exposed bust screams PG-13, so I remove the Christmas pin from the lapel of my jacket and use it to close the lower V of her cleavage. "Just don't bend over," I instruct.

She rolls her eyes. "You're no fun."

Her makeup is as flamboyant as she is, so I draw her to the tiny table I have my tools on and smudge off the gloss on her lips with a tissue. "This would be great for the theater show, but for tonight, we want you to be understated so you don't show up Santa."

She'll do anything for Uncle Odin but still complains. "Behind every successful man is a confident woman."

My uncle winks at her. "So true," he agrees.

Her extravagant eyeshadow is more difficult to subdue. The sparkles she's spread generously over the lids and under the brows won't come off without remover. I don't have time to completely redo the look, so I leave it alone and blend out her blush, subtly contouring her cheeks.

Next, I snatch up my brush to tame her lively curls. Normally, I love to see her with her hair down, but tonight, the effect is too sexy along with the rest of her. Gently brushing the locks up and away from her face, I make a sassy pony on the top of her head, allowing the curls to cascade like a fountain. I insert snowflake clips to control a few wayward wisps and she looks years younger.

"Wow," she says, eyeing herself in the handheld mirror I extend. She touches her hair and shakes her head gently, watching the curls sway. "You're good at this."

I poke her side at the dig. "I get my artistic ability, glamour, and love of color from you, but sometimes, a little understatement actually works wonders."

"I think you look lovely, my dear," Uncle Odin says.

She tweaks his beard. "Thank you, Odin. Or should I say Santa Claus?"

As I tuck my supplies and tools away, she tugs on one of my braids. "Your hair seems calmer tonight. Are you handling things better or did you spell it?"

I've woven silver and blue ribbons into the plaits of my natural color, trying to look festive without putting on the horrible Christmas sweater Belle suggested I wear. The ribbons and pin, which Matilda now brandishes, were as jolly as I could get. At least it was something, though. "No spell. I'm fine."

A skeptical look passes over her face, but she lets it go. "It was good of you to find a replacement angel and take Sawyer to help. How did that all go?"

"Better than I anticipated," I tell her honestly, stuffing my makeup bag with the brushes and zipping it closed.

"Friends again?"

She's digging for more. "Friendly, anyway."

"Sawyer's a good boy," Uncle Odin chimes in. "But you're right to take it slow."

"Thank you." I lean over and hug him. "I appreciate the support. I also know that all of you are pushing us together, so you can stop pretending it's a coincidence that Leo had to meet with an out-of-town client and couldn't go dig for the angel himself, and that Sawyer just happened to be assisting you with that costume when he dropped in this afternoon." I look between them. "I'm not that dense."

Uncle Odin squeezes my arm and grins. "It's great fun trying to pull one over on you."

Matilda smacks his big belly. "Hush, elf boy. Don't give away our secrets."

"Sure wish we had some snow." Nonni bursts in with Poppi on her heels. She's carrying two trays of cookies to enter in the contest. "My, don't you all look…" Her gaze lands on Matilda and her brows draw down. "Fabulous."

Matilda does a twirl. "Why, thank you."

Poppi's eyes bug out and I stop her spin, halfway through. "Yeah, don't do that. Don't bend over. Don't twirl. Got it?"

Another eye roll. "Party poopers."

Belle has the giant bay doors at the front of the building open, and tables line the walls. Five impressive gingerbread houses take up one designated for the adult entries, and another dozen smaller versions are stationed on a second for the children's. In front of each is a placard with the name of the designer.

The Ladies' Garden Club is hosting the cookie contest and trays of samples are laid out on the other tables. The town gets to vote on their favorites, unlike the gingerbread houses, which are judged by more official means.

"We better get you signed in," Poppi says to Nonni, navigating both of them around Uncle Odin. "You guys have fun and let us know if you need help with anything."

"Good luck," I tell Nonni. "No matter who wins, I'm happy to take any leftovers off your hands."

She winks and they leave us to join the crowd out front.

Once the winners are announced, Uncle Odin will take his place on a raised platform with an elaborate chair that looks like a throne. Kids will line up to tell him their wish list and get their pictures taken with him.

"The angel looks nice." Matilda points to the door, peering out the glass top.

Across the center of downtown, City Hall and both trees are lit up. Main Street is closed off and vendors and craftspeople have booths lining the street, selling their baked products and handmade gifts. Snow has her stand selling apple products and cider once again, and Broden is managing the petting zoo of miniature farm animals at the park.

All up and down the road, shop owners are hosting sidewalk sales, and many display Christmas quilts in their front windows for the town to see. Nonni's now proudly hangs in one of ours, and Cinder and Finn are manning our sale table. Since most of us are involved in tonight's event, we decided to close the store, but participate in the sidewalk sale.

"It's not quite as big as the previous one, but it'll do," I comment.

My gaze drops to two men standing behind the angel tree. They both have cups of cider from Snow's apple stand. There's no mistaking Leo's giant build; Sawyer's either. For a moment, my heart feels all warm and fuzzy, knowing Sawyer has found a friend or two here again. He never did have many, and the couple he hung with moved away after high school. I hadn't thought much about it, but I'm one of the few still here.

The square bell rings and folks begin to move toward the station as Belle announces it's time for the gingerbread house contest. As I peek from the back to watch Ruby, Ren, and Minerva surveying the lovely houses, Sawyer appears at my shoulder, startling me. "What I would give to eat every one of those," he says.

"You always had a sweet tooth."

He offers me a steaming cup of cider. "Brought you something."

It's warm and spicy, just the way I like it. I enjoy his banter with Uncle Odin and Matilda until the winner is announced and the crowd cheers.

Next up is the children's contest. I don't envy Ruby having to judge. She'll make one youngster very happy, but the rest will be sad.

Knowing my sister, however, they'll all walk away with some sort of present for entering. That's just how she is, always bringing cheer, like Belle, to everyone she can.

"Hey, I wanted to show you this." Sawyer holds up a gold bracelet with a charm on it. "When I moved the boom to put the new angel on the tree, it fell out. It must have been caught on one of the bars or the stairs. Do you think it belongs to our thief?"

The charm is a medallion with a figure in robes and a halo-like hat. "Looks like a Catholic saint. You should give it to Robyn."

Leo enters through the side door. "How's it going? Need anything?"

"We're fine," I tell him. "Thank you for sharing the angel with the town."

He notices the bracelet. "That's an oldie."

"You've seen one of these before?" Sawyer asks.

He studies the figure. "Sure. This is Saint Nicholas of Marian, the patron saint of children. This particular design is probably from the 1930s or 40s."

Sawyer inspects it once more. "Saint Nicholas, like... Santa Claus?"

Out in the main area, Ruby announces a twelve-way tie for first place in the children's gingerbread contest. The gathered townsfolk go crazy, clapping and hooting, and I smile at her cleverness.

"Oh yes," Uncle Odin points at the medal, "Saint Nick, patron saint to sailors, children, and one of several legends who distributed gifts to kids around the world in December."

Belle waits for the applause to die down before she speaks into the mic. "And now what you've all been waiting for!"

Fresh cheers and applause fill the station as she pauses to build the excitement. "The one and only Santa Claus!"

Her voice is nearly drowned out before she finishes and my smile broadens. I'm glad to be here tonight, feeling a rush of Christmas spirit.

"Come on, Nick." Matilda winks at Uncle Odin. "Time to spread some holiday cheer."

Belle has lined up Shelby and Cody once again to assist Matilda in handing out candy canes to those who've come to see Santa.

Uncle Odin is a natural and even the shyest child warms to him. Some days, I think he's just a big kid himself, so seeing him in this role is heart-warming.

The town votes on the cookies and Nonni wins second place with her animal sugar cookies, each one resembling one of our pets decked out in holiday colors. Once that contest is done, folks start purchasing the treats. The hedgehogs sell out first, but I'm happy to see the ferret cookies, with their red scarves, are a hit, too.

Making sure we get some, Sawyer and I mill around munching on them, me keeping an eye on my uncle and godmother. The tone is jovial and most folks speak to us and wish us a Merry Christmas. Plenty are still upset about the stolen angel, but I notice dozens of them over at City Hall, adding their wishes to the tree.

Minerva catches me staring at it. "That gives so many hope. It's been a hard year in this town. I hope everyone's wishes come true."

When the last child is on Uncle Odin's lap, I text Robyn and tell her about the bracelet. She's patrolling Main Street and the park, but asks us to meet her at her office at nine.

Sawyer, Ren, Leo, and I are cleaning up Santa's throne and loading the chair in Ren's pick-up truck when Belle rushes out to us. I immediately go on high alert when I see her face. "What's wrong?"

"One of the gingerbread houses is gone."

"Gone?" Matilda and Uncle Odin have already left for home, and Belle lowered the bay doors several minutes ago. The remaining crowd is milling around downtown and buying last-minute gifts at the park.

"What do you mean?" Ren asks.

"It's gone! Holly is here from the paper to take a picture for the article in tomorrow's holiday addition, and the winning house by Adele Bingham is missing."

Ruby scans the vehicles nearby. "Did she take it home already?"

"Adele is in there. In tears, I might add." Belle points to the station. "I was helping clean up cookie containers and I brought a load out to Franny's car. Adele was in the restroom, fixing her makeup for the photo. No one else was inside. Holly had been at the angel tree and when I walked her in to set up for the photo, the gingerbread house had disappeared."

Ren, too, glances around. "Who would steal that?"

"Who *could* steal a big thing like that out from under our noses?" Ruby clarifies.

Sawyer meets my eyes. "Looks like our thief has struck again."

# TWELVE

"I'll report it to Robyn," I tell Belle. "You guys stay here and finish up."

Sawyer comes with me to the police station. Snow calls out as we pass her booth. She's covering the table with a cloth, since the downtown walk will be another opportunity to sell her products. "You look like two people on a mission. Did Nonni win?"

"I'll catch you up later," I call. "We have to meet with Robyn."

"Is everything okay?"

"Our thief may have stolen the winning gingerbread house," Sawyer tells her.

"Oh no! That's terrible."

We keep going and find Robyn at her desk. Her decorations are slim, but she does have a fresh miniature tree on the corner. "You're early," she says.

Across from her is Rain, looking comfortable in a guest chair. "Hi, Zelle." He stands and nods at me, while offering a hand to Sawyer. "You're Minerva's grandson, right? I'm Marion Redfern. Friends call me Rain."

Sawyer shakes his hand. "Nice to meet you."

"We're sorry to crash the party," I say to my cousin, "but the winning gingerbread house is missing. We think someone stole it while we were cleaning up."

She shakes her head, her shoulders tensing. "What is happening in our town?"

"I'll get out of your hair," Rain says, moving for the door. "Let me know if there's anything I can do to help. See you tomorrow?"

His puppy dog eyes hold hers. She gives him an encouraging smile. "Lunch?"

His face lights up. "Text me when you're available. I'll bring it to you."

After he scoots out, I turn to her. "That seems to be going well."

She waves me into the chair he vacated. A tinge of pink blooms on her cheeks. "He's a nice guy. We're friends, that's all."

"Of course." I wink at Sawyer as he sits next to me. "He is. We all really like him."

She eyes me over her computer as she grabs the handset of the landline and punches a button. "Don't get any ideas. You know I'm too busy to date."

I press my lips together and give her my innocent face. "Who said anything about dating?"

She chuckles, seeing right through me. The person on the other end answers. "Sorry, Reid. I know you're off, but I'm short-handed and we've had another incident."

Reid responds and she hangs up. Her fingers dash over her keyboard. "So first, tell me what happened with the gingerbread house. Then we'll get to the bracelet."

The station is dead quiet, only the sound of my voice as I relate the details, and her typing, can be heard. Sawyer says nothing, but his solid presence beside me feels good.

Robyn uses her mouse and then puts her fingers back on the keys. "Explain where everyone was again right before Belle noticed it was gone."

I start explaining, but Sawyer says, "Here, I'll show you."

Using items on Robyn's desk, he fashions a miniature station from them, using pens from her holder to stand in for the people. "We were here," he tells her, indicating the parking lot. "As far as we know, the only person inside at the time was Adele. She was in the restroom at the rear." He places a pen in the appropriate location.

"Could the thief have been hiding inside?" Robyn asks.

Sawyer and I exchange a glance. "I suppose so," I answer. "It is a big place. There are plenty of areas someone could conceal themselves, but wouldn't we have seen them carrying it out?"

"Not if they went through the side door." Sawyer stands and stares down on the improvised layout and where all of us were at the time. He points to the exit that looks out at downtown and the building we're in. "No one was over there, and if any passersby noticed someone carrying it out, they probably assumed it was just a contestant taking it home."

"Basically, we have no idea who it might have been or why they would take it," Robyn states, also scrutinizing the items. "But we might get lucky and find a witness who did see the culprit. A long shot, but we have to start somewhere."

We study the desk as she finishes typing up a report. The front door opens and closes and Officer Reid sticks his head in. "I was downtown at the sales with my wife. We did a quick search of Main Street and I questioned all the vendors, but no one saw anything."

"Check the security footage from here and City Hall. If the thief went out the side door of the station, we may have caught them on camera."

Reid disappears and I mentally cross my fingers. I don't hold out much hope, but like Robyn said, it's a start. Problem is, even if they show up, the distance is so far, we may not get a good image.

"The old fire station doesn't have active cameras on it anymore," she tells us, "since it's only used for community events now. I'm wishing it did."

"Do you think the thief knew that?" I tap my chin. "Like they knew about the ones at City Hall?"

"I can already see tomorrow's headline in the paper," Sawyer tells us. "'Angel Thief Strikes Again.'"

Robyn nods. "Anything's possible, and it does seem like they're related. Smart criminal, it seems. Speaking of, show me this bracelet."

Sawyer withdraws it from his pocket and explains how he found it. "Could belong to the person who stole the angel."

"Or anyone in town." Robyn counters. "While the fact it fell off the boom indicates it came from someone who may have been crawling around on there, it's not exactly concrete evidence."

Sawyer isn't buying that. "With all due respect, detective, this is a solid lead. We find who owns it, and I bet dollars to donuts, we find our perpetrator."

She looks at him as though he's been watching too many episodes of *Law and Order*. "I wish things were that clear cut." She yawns and hands it back. "It's part of my job to play devil's advocate. The owner could have misplaced or dropped it, and a bird, squirrel, or other animal might have found it and carried it onto the equipment. A past operator may have lost it. There are dozens of possibilities."

I see Sawyer tense as if he's prepared to argue, and I intercept his challenge. "But you are going to look into our theory, right?"

"Sure." She rocks back in her chair, appearing as if she'd rather be at home in bed. "But there are nearly four thousand adults in this town, over fifty percent are female. Any one of them could own that, and even if it does belong to our larcenist, I still can't get a warrant to search anyone's residence based on that."

Feeling slightly defeated, I stand. "I'm going to keep it, then, and start asking around. Maybe I can find the owner."

Her brow furrows. "Be careful, Zelle. If you do, contact me immediately, okay?"

"You think the person's dangerous?" Sawyer asks. "I mean, we're talking about a Christmas tree topper and a gingerbread house. Doesn't seem like a violent criminal."

"Better safe than sorry," she tells us, rising. She walks us to the entrance. "I'll call Adele and see if she remembers anything else, like someone who seemed overly interested in her house. You reassure Belle for me. I'll catch the thief, I promise."

Sawyer and I say goodnight to her and stand on the concrete steps. The stars are bright overhead, the air frosty. Downtown has cleared for the most part, the last of the booths closed up. Lights are out at the station, and the news van is gone.

Sawyer holds up the bracelet and the gold glimmers in the illumination from the streetlamp. "So what now? How do we find who this belongs to?"

I gaze at the two lighted trees of City Hall. "We don't."

Down the block, his grandmother's shop windows glow with Christmas lights, displaying several of the quilts her group has made. "You're giving up?"

"No." I smile and grab his arm, tugging him down Main Street. "I have a plan. Come on."

# THIRTEEN

"Someone has seen this bracelet and knows who it belongs to," I say. "All we need is to find them."

Inside the mansion, we find Cinder working on the downstairs fireplace, cleaning the flue in preparation for our Christmas morning celebration.

While the formerly dormant hearth is in the remodeled section of the shop, we've found we like using it during non-store hours. We've decorated the mantle with holly, mistletoe, and a variety of pine branches, and Belle wound tiny fairy lights around the garland.

"Belle's freaking out about the thefts," Cinder tells us, wiping her ash-smudged hands on a towel. "Does Robyn have any leads?"

"Nothing yet." I allow Sawyer to help me off with my coat. "Where is Belle?"

"Here." She steps out from the turret doorway, Leo on her heels. "What did she say?"

I lay the coat over my arm. "She has an officer reviewing camera footage and we think the culprit snuck it out the side door. She plans to question anyone in that vicinity at the time who might have witnessed it."

Belle's shoulders slump. "This is a disaster. Adele is so disappointed."

I squeeze her arm. "We'll get it back." *I hope.* "And the angel. You'll see."

Cinder places a log in the hearth. "Does Robyn think the disappearances are related?"

Sawyer hands her another from the pile waiting on the floor. "Possibly, but there's no proof."

"Of course they are." Belle's voice is filled with frustration and exasperation. "Two items in two days, both connected to our event? How could they not be?"

"Do you think someone is trying to sabotage Christmas in Story Cove?" Cinder asks.

Leo leans on the back of a chair. "Why would anyone want to do that?"

We fall silent for a moment, considering it. Cinder places the last log on the arrangement and steps back. "I don't know, but I, too, believe they have to be. Maybe Finn's investigator will be able to figure something out."

"I sure hope so." Belle lets Leo draw her to his chest. "What a nightmare this is."

"You need some sleep." He rubs her back and she closes her eyes. "You've been running yourself ragged."

"He's right," Cinder agrees. "Go to bed, Belle. We'll all do what we can to find the stolen items first thing tomorrow."

Leo leaves and Belle retires. Cinder calls Finn to update him. Ruby is out with Ren, and Uncle Odin and Matilda have already gone to their rooms.

I take Sawyer to our personal kitchen and put the kettle on to heat.

He shrugs off his jacket and hangs it on the back of a chair before he pulls it out to sit. "You didn't tell them about the bracelet."

"I didn't want to get Belle's hopes up." I grab two of the Santa mugs in the dish drainer. "Tea, cocoa, or eggnog?"

"Cocoa." I should have known; it was always his favorite. "Robyn could be right and it's not connected to the angel."

I open the door of our antique pie safe and retrieve a container of decorated sugar cookies. "She may also be wrong. It's one of the only leads we have and you and I are going to pursue it."

"The owner could be our thief." Sawyer watches me arrange several on a plate, then snags one as I set the plate on the table.

"Exactly." I spoon cocoa into the mugs. "And you and I have the perfect connections to this town's movers and shakers. We're tapped into the gossip network."

"We are?"

I splash milk into the cups and microwave them. "Yes, we are. Me through my clients, you through the quilt shop."

He finishes the treat in two more bites. "Why don't we put up some found signs around town with your number on them?"

"Because if our pilferer discovers she lost it while stealing the angel, and realizes we're onto her, she won't come forward."

He nods. "How will the gossip network help?"

The microwave dings. I remove the cups from it and stir. "We show the ladies a picture of it and ask if anyone recognizes who it belongs to, see if anyone can point us in the right direction."

He eyes another cookie. "What if we show it to the thief accidentally?"

The kettle whistles and I add a portion of hot water to each of the cups. "You'll know by their reaction."

"But then they'll know we're wise to them."

I plunk the cocoa in front of him. "Yes, but at least we'll know who to keep an eye on while we gather evidence for Robyn to arrest them."

He stares at the Santa mug. "No marshmallows?"

I sigh and pick through the pantry until I find some. He thanks me when I plop several into his drink.

"Even if I agree to sacrifice myself and hang out with the quilting club ladies, that's only a couple dozen women. This town probably has, what? Two hundred or more?"

I snag two candy canes and add them to our beverages. "*Only*? Are you serious? These are women who thrive on being in the know. Combined with my clients, I bet we'll have an answer to the Saint Nick medal by Christmas Eve, if not before."

"Bet, huh?" He drags out a twenty from his wallet and slaps it on the table. "I'll take that wager."

He's trying to draw me into a challenge like we used to have. He thinks he's so smart, but I've got news for him. I lift my mug in salute. "You're going to lose."

He grins but looks pained at the same time. "You really want me to hang out at the quilt shop tomorrow?"

I set my cocoa down, enjoying the fear in his eyes. I begin undoing my braid, laying the ribbons on the table and scratching at my scalp. "Absolutely."

"You're a sadist."

Grinning, I shake out the last of my plaited hair, and catch him watching. Feeling heat on my cheeks, I bite into a sugar cookie, and avoid his smile.

The icing melts on my tongue. I've already had too much sugar and caffeine, so it'll probably be another sleepless night. "If we don't get a hit tomorrow, we'll walk around at the Jingle Bell Jam in the evening and ask folks there. Someone is bound to recognize it."

He watches me lick the icing from my lips, drumming his fingers. "What's that?"

"Belle came up with a new charity event for the year. There's a downtown walk, toy drive, and pet photo booth. Everyone gets a stocking stuffed with coupons to use at the shops, and they're asked to give whatever they save to the two charities the town council voted on to support this year— Santa's Toy Sack or Paws-4-Ever."

He takes the last cookie, a Christmas tree, and points the end at me. "Only for you, would I subject myself to the quilters. They're absolutely rabid."

"Your sacrifice is duly noted." I sip my drink. "I really do appreciate it, by the way. It kills me to see Belle so upset. I can't let her down."

His phone rings. "It's Mamaw."

I nod for him to answer and listen as he attempts to calm her down. She's already heard about the gingerbread house and is quite upset. I hear her voice through the phone.

When he's finally assured her there's nothing she can do and he'll be home soon, he disconnects and sucks up a marshmallow. "Belle's not the only one up in arms, and as my grandmother just reminded me, this is still my hometown. I'm happy to help, and the bracelet is a clue, I'd bet on it."

I really do feel better having him help me with this. We stare at each other for a long moment. My insides do a little flip at his steady gaze. "Thank you," I manage to squeak out.

He rises, gulps down the rest of the cocoa, and winks. "Thanks for the treats, Rebel."

After he leaves, I force myself to sit and finish mine, reviewing everything that's happened in the past two days.

Then I go downstairs to ask my oldest sister for advice.

# FOURTEEN

"Need any help?" I ask.

Like all of us, Cinder is not the needy type. She's independent and a touch stubborn. She would never ask for assistance making candles.

Being the eldest, she also senses my need to chat. "Sure. Come on in."

A pot of wax melts on the stove in the commercial kitchen. She's set out a large bottle of scent and a container of colored chips. The dozen glass jars need wicks, so I grab the bag of cotton ones and begin peeling off the stickers to secure them to the jar bottoms.

All is quiet and serene. I almost hate to break the comfortable silence, so I let it stretch, enjoying this time with her.

Our parents reared us all to be independent, yet value our family bond. Although Belle and I are not identical, our mom and dad made sure we explored and understood our individual identities, as well as our gifts.

As I prep the glass holders, I think about those talents that differentiate, as well as unite, us.

While Belle can hear books talk to her, my magick is odder. Being able to color my hair at will is hardly an amazing skill, although most who know about it believe it is. Cinder can literally step into someone's shoes and know things about them. Ruby has her red cape that heals, and while her other skills are weaker, she can use her magick to do things like organize our office and even freeze people when called for.

Right now, Cinder doesn't need to step into my shoes to know I'm searching for some sisterly advice. She stirs the melting wax. "How are things with Sawyer?"

"Fine. How's the chimney?"

"There was actually quite a bit of gunk in there. I think we should switch to using the seasoned oak." She measures out the scent. "What's the temp?"

I use our heat gun to check. "Just right," I say, sounding like Goldilocks. Switching the burner off, I move the pot to a cooling rack and keep stirring.

"What are you and Sawyer up to?"

My hair is down to my ankles, the heavy weight tugging on my scalp. I can't wait to shave it off before bed. Some days are like that. While I normally enjoy feeling it around me at night, like a security blanket, other times I need to be free of it. "Just tracking down our thief."

"I'm sure Robyn will appreciate that, but what can you two do that she can't?"

"I may have a lead." Crossing my fingers seems childish, but I do it anyway. "It may not pan out, though, so I don't want to tell Belle until it does."

"What kind of lead? It's nothing dangerous, is it?"

I laugh. "Not at all. It's telling that you would jump to that conclusion."

Her smile is motherly. "You're not one to think before you act, but that's not why I asked. I worry about all of you. It's out of concern, not an assumption you'll leap into something risky."

Sure. I wink at her. "You worry too much. I made it to this age, so even if I'm a bit impulsive, I must have good instincts, right?"

It's her turn to laugh. "I suppose. Or you've got an understanding guardian angel."

Mom. It's what we're both thinking, even though neither of us says it.

She pours the liquid scent into a measuring glass and eyeballs the amount. "You and Sawyer seem to getting along now."

I stop stirring and check the temperature once more. Not cool enough to add the scent just yet. "Yes, but..."

"But what?"

"It's complicated."

Using a scoop, she gathers enough tinted chips for

this weight of product and hands it to me. "Have you discussed why he left?"

I add the coloring and mix it in well. The pretty Christmas red will darken once the candles set. I clean the spoon and stick it in the drainer to dry, then lean against the counter. I toy with a lock of my hair, wrapping it around my wrist.

My magick has turned it a frosted blue and I rather like it. A part of me is relieved it's not doing that rainbow effect that Sawyer seems to bring on. "He left town because of his mother. What's there to discuss?"

Cinder's look drills into my heart. "He was trying to keep a connection with her. I can't say I blame him. He wanted to help her out after her husband left her high and dry."

And there it is...the lecture. Well-intended, yet still making me feel like a teenager again. "I know."

Sawyer's mom has always been childlike, never learning how to fend for herself in the world, and always needing someone—usually a man—to take care of her. An idea I can't wrap my brain around, being as independent as I am. I know that even Minerva is confused by her daughter's behavior because as a young widow, she had to be self-sufficient as well as self-supporting.

Unfortunately, Sawyer ends up picking up the pieces when the latest boyfriend or husband leaves Janice. "I don't blame her," I tell my sister. "I also know he was being a good son. But he stayed away from here because he's a chicken."

She takes the spoon and adds the scent. A warm chocolate-peppermint aroma fills the air. "Why do you say that?"

"He said I was better off without him, bailed, then never responded to my texts or calls. Rescuing his mother was a convenient excuse for him to leave me and not commit to our future."

A frustrated frown contracts her features. "He loves you, Zelle. You and his grandmother were the only people he could ever count on."

"Exactly, but I counted on him, too. Plus, he has a fear of commitment."

She hands me the measuring cup to wash. "Let me guess, you did a spell to ascertain that truth?"

*Busted.* Out of all of us, I embrace potion-making much more freely than my sisters. "I did a few months after he was gone. I kept believing he'd eventually return and we'd pick up where we'd left off. Not so. The spell revealed his fears."

While she pours the wax, I settle into a chair near the fireplace. Rumpelstiltskin hops into my lap and offers me a ribbon for my hair. I nuzzle his tiny face as a thanks, then gather up the heavy strands. Once secured, I let it cascade over my left shoulder. He paws at the silky material.

Cinder sets the pot in the sink. "I understand how much he hurt you. It's okay to be conflicted about his return."

I do love my big sister. She wants to tell me to get over it and give him a second chance, but she's trying to be diplomatic. "Conflicted is putting it mildly. He has a tattoo." I keep my tone light. "It reads, 'Rebel.'"

She turns to face me. "You've got to be kidding. He showed you?"

"Not intentionally. I happened to catch him working at the amphitheater and saw it."

Her brows lower into a classic Cinder look. "So he *is* still in love with you."

I pick at the ribbon and let Rumpelstiltskin rub his cheek on my hair. "Does it matter? I guess that's what I need advice about. Love may not be enough, and there's a lot of water under the bridge. He has a phobia about commitment, partially because of his mom, I think. He's never seen her happy or in a stable relationship. I have a lot of forgiving to do, but how do I trust him not to run off again?"

She offers a patient, cajoling smile. "If there's one thing we have in common, sister, it's our skepticism. While that spell revealed his fear of commitment, that was years ago. Have you done one this week? People change, you know."

Scooping up the ferret, I stand and break eye contact. "No."

"And why not?"

I force myself to meet her gaze once more, my heart a wounded mess of hope. "Because either way—whether he loves me or not—I'm screwed."

"I don't believe that." She puts an arm around me and I rest my head on her shoulder. "It's the season for miracles, Zelle. Give him a chance, and see what happens."

"I'm scared," I whisper. "What if he breaks my heart again?"

She gives me a supportive, big sister squeeze. "What if he doesn't?" she whispers back.

CHAPTER

# FIFTEEN

I've just gone to sleep when a loud banging sends me sitting straight up. "What the...?"

Rumpelstiltskin hops into my lap and reaches up to touch my face. I wonder for a moment if I've imagined the noise, and rub his head, reassuring him. I was in the middle of a crazy dream about drowning in a cauldron of Christmas lights while Sawyer simply smiled down at me.

I rub my eyes and yawn. "Just a dream," I tell my ferret.

The blankets are warm as I tuck him under with me and begin to settle in once more, my racing heart still thudding in my chest.

*Bang, bang, bang!*

I jerk upright again and Rumpel high-tails it off the bed. Jayne barks from my sister's room. Out in the hall, scuffling commences as the others stir.

Scrambling to grab my robe, I wrap it around me before I open my door to find a sleepy Belle coming out of her room across from me. Jayne dashes down the stairs.

"What's going on?" I ask.

She shrugs. Matilda throws open her door, her hair secured on top of her head in a messy bun and a mint green face mask covering her skin. "Someone's at the front."

Cinder and Ruby join us. "Who could it be at this time of night?" Cinder yawns.

"Robyn?" Belle suggests.

"She would have called first," Ruby says.

A squeak from the door at the end of the hall warns that Uncle Odin is also awake. "I believe we have company," he announces with a good-natured smile. "Perhaps we should let them in."

"Maybe Santa needs a stand-in." Belle winks at him. "Or he's come early to ask for your help on Christmas Eve."

He plays along, returning her wink. "He probably wishes to order chocolates from Ruby."

Cinder starts for the stairs, not one to play games. "I'll see who it is."

Ruby is two steps behind. "I'm coming with you."

"We're all going," Matilda states, motioning at me and Belle.

I'm so sleepy, I sway on my feet. Belle entwines her arm through mine and leads me down, Uncle Odin bringing up the rear.

Another knock comes from the entrance, followed by a voice. "Tilly? Are you here?"

Cinder flips on the shop light and looks back at our godmother. "Tilly?"

Matilda's eyes have gone wide. "Oh dear."

"Oh dear, what?" Ruby queries. "Who is it?"

Matilda motions Cinder to the side. "No one. You all go back to bed. I'll handle this."

"Don't be silly, my dear." Uncle Odin heads for the door. "We should welcome Cherisse. It's been a long time."

She grabs his wrist to keep him from reaching the handle. "It has been a long time. A very, very long time. I'll see what she wants, and then send her on her way."

"Who's Cherisse?" I question here. "And why don't you want us to meet her?"

"A lovely person," Uncle Odin tells me. "She must have traveled a great distance to be here."

The five of us stare at Matilda, silently demanding an explanation.

She sighs and lifts her hands palms-up in the air. "Oh for goddess' sake." Her fingers flip the lock and she grips the knob tightly. "Just remember I offered."

Cold air rushes in as she swings the door open. A woman dressed in leather boots up to her thighs and a flashy green jacket that comes down to the tops of the black leather steps inside. She carries a fabric hobo bag and wears a knit cap. "Tilly!" Her arms go around Matilda's neck. "I knew you were playing possum! It's so good to see you."

Our godmother hesitantly pats her back. "And you, sort of."

The woman squeal-laughs and takes Matilda by the shoulders. "Same ol' Tilly."

She rounds on us, her green cat eyes looking each of us over. "And you must be the Sherwood sisters. I've heard so much about you."

"Wish we could say the same," Cinder remarks, one brow raised at Matilda. "I take it you're a friend of our godmother?"

"A friend?" Her eyes snap and her mouth curves in a Cheshire grin. She glances at Matilda. "You didn't tell them?"

"Tell us what?" I question.

A heavy sigh leaves Matilda's lips. "Girls, this is Cherisse." She closes and locks the door. "She's my sister."

THE NEXT MORNING I leave my hair natural again, and trim it into a bob. It looks odd to me, the alternating gold, silver, and white strands still foreign after years of coloring it, yet it takes me back to happier times.

Matilda and Cherisse disappeared into the tower after last night's announcement, and I wonder if they'll be at breakfast together. If her sister is here for the holidays. Belle and I whispered about this surprise guest well into the morning, and she attempted to quiz Uncle Odin, but he insisted the story was Matilda's to tell.

I take a picture of the bracelet and send it to Sawyer so he can start querying the quilters today at the shop. He texts back a photo of a man being mobbed by older women.

At breakfast, Belle comments about my look. "Going *au naturel*, huh? I like it. We haven't seen this style since..."

Her face blanches when I glance up. Since Sawyer left— the words hang in the air.

Matilda and Cherisse are absent. Ruby pulls cinnamon bread from the oven and Uncle Odin sips his orange juice. "Seems like you two are getting along again," he says.

His smile is benign, but I see the twinkle in his eyes.

"It's no big deal," I tell the group, noticing both Cinder and Ruby are eyeing me with knowing grins on their lips. "We're friends, period. I've been hard on him since he came back, but please remember, he's not staying forever."

"Who isn't?" Cherisse sweeps in, wearing leggings under her boots, along with a festive silk blouse. She's braided her hair on the left side and adorned it with tinsel strands. They flash under the overhead light, much like her eyes.

"A friend of mine," I tell her.

She winks as if she's in on who Sawyer is. "A good one, I bet."

My cheeks heat for some ridiculous reason.

Matilda breezes in after her, her glittering earrings matching her flamboyant Christmas sweater. Two cartoon reindeer look as though they might fly right off the cotton front, wreaths of decorated garlands around their necks. "He broke her heart four years ago," she tells her sister.

"Ah." Cherisse takes an empty chair. "That kind of friend."

Discussing my private life with her feels discomfiting. Ruby offers the plate of sliced bread to me, steam rising from it, and I'm grateful for the distraction.

Matilda serves her sister a cup of coffee and Cherisse helps herself to a slice as well. I pass a bowl of cut up fruit to them, and Cherisse butters her bread.

A tense silence fills the room, all waiting to see if either of the two women are going to fill us in on what Cherisse is doing here and how long she plans to stay.

They eat in silence.

Belle can't stand it. "So Cherisse, what brings you to town?"

She swallows a mouthful and uses a manicured finger to wipe a bit of butter from the corner of her lips. "I came to spend Christmas with my little sister, of course. And call me Rissy. Everyone does."

Tilly and Rissy. "Are you a Valkyrie?" I inquire.

Her green eyes look at me from under her brows. That Cheshire grin returns. "Of course, sugar."

"It's Zelle."

She nods, sipping her coffee. "Love the hair. Tilly tells me you do amazing things with it."

We've gone from one subject to a second that I don't wish to discuss. "Those boots are really something."

She takes the redirect with grace, enjoying conversational wave turning herself. "With proper boots, all doors open."

Belle and I exchange a glance. "Are you a fairytale lover?" my twin asks.

She winks at her. "Aren't we all?"

Matilda sets down her fork. "Well, I'd like to hear names of potential suspects for the stolen angel and gingerbread house, Belle."

"I wish I had some," she replies. "Has anyone heard from Robyn yet?"

We all shake our heads. "Don't worry," I insist, cleaning up my place and taking my dishes to the sink. "Everything's going to work out, I promise."

She smiles at me, but I can see her doubt. "Thank you, Zelle."

I hug her. Rissy turns to Matilda and elbows her. "That's how sisters are supposed to treat each other."

Our godmother rolls her eyes and crams her mouth with bread.

Before I leave, she catches up with me. "Don't pay any attention to Rissy. She can be a handful, but she means well."

Sounds like what I might say about her. "Is there a reason you didn't mention her to us?"

"A million." She hands me my hat. "Have a good day."

MY SCHEDULE at the salon is filled with women getting styled for Christmas. Most are having big gatherings, and that means pressure to look their best.

The energy is high, and there's a lot of talk about what they're wearing, what food they're making, and how many guests will be at their house. I listen, nod, and comment as necessary, feeling a bit swept up in the planning and excitement.

The three other stylists have the same type of clients. Sometimes, we even exchange knowing glances when two or more of them attempt to outdo each other. Thank goodness we have to shampoo and put them under dryers at certain points to stop an all-out competition from erupting.

A few of mine are adventurous with their cut and styles, and I add frosted tints, red low lights, and even craft a cool Christmas tree loop braid for my former English teacher, Mrs. Crumm. She's hosting a party tonight and is delighted to have her hair be a showpiece.

Before each one leaves, I make sure to show them the picture I took of the bracelet, but none have any clue about it.

Around three, Lovey Conroy arrives with Nonni in tow. My hair is down past my hips and Nonni is delighted that's it's all natural today. Lovey's bad hip makes it a challenge for her to get into my chair, so Nonni and I help her.

Once she's comfortable, I get each a cup of coffee from our kitchenette in the back. Lovey and I discuss touching up her roots, as well as trimming her dry ends.

Once I have her colored and under the dryer, I show Nonni the picture.

"I used to have one of these," she tells me. "I probably still do in one of my jewelry boxes."

"You do?"

"The ladies auxiliary did a fundraiser when I was just a girl. They gave these out."

"So it *is* old."

She gives me the stink eye. "That was back in the forties, so yes, I guess you could say that."

I stumble over myself to get on her good side again. "You're ageless, timeless, and I love you."

She hugs me and all is well once more. "What do you think about this Cherisse gal?"

"Not sure yet. She's quirky like Matilda, but in a different way."

Nonni thinks that over. "Wonder why Matilda kept her a secret?"

I've been hashing that over myself. "There's definitely bad blood between them. I didn't realize Matilda had any relatives."

I finish Lovey's hair. Nonni asks her if she remembers the bracelets, and she does. "Lost mine a long time ago," she tells me. "Why are you looking for one of those?"

"Oh, I found this on the sidewalk the other day. Belle's boyfriend, Leo, said it was pretty old, but I've no idea who it belongs to."

"There are dozens of women our age in town who may have received one back then," Nonni tells me and Lovey nods her agreement.

"Any chance you could tell me who?"

Between the two of them, they rattle off dozens of possibilities, and I make a list. "This is great. Thank you," I offer as I walk them out.

I don't have any more time to worry about the daunting list until Sawyer comes in at closing time. "I may have a lead," he tells me as a greeting.

"I may have a dozen or more."

He looks surprised. "Mamaw has a bracelet just like the one I found, can you believe it?"

"Half the women over sixty do." I sigh in frustration. "At least they did at one time, according to Nonni. She has one too."

"Mamaw said that Betsy McCallahan wears hers all the time."

That gets my attention. Betsy owns the coffee shop three blocks over. What are the odds it belongs to her?

I hurriedly finish my cleanup and grab my coat. "Looks like you're buying me a coffee."

CHAPTER
# SIXTEEN

Betsy's closing The Perking Pot when we arrive, the last of her customers carrying out a variety of baked goods, roasted beans, and a few coffee-related gift items.

"We're sorry to bother you," Sawyer says after we meet her at the door. "We need to ask you a question."

"I heard you were back in town," she says to him, motioning us to come in. Her keen eyes look him up and down. "About time you came back to take care of your grandma."

He smiles, full of southern charm. "Yes, ma'am. It's been too long."

She locks up and starts putting chairs on the tables. We help. "What is it you two need?"

Removing the bracelet from my jacket pocket, I hold it up in the light for her to see. "Do you recognize this?"

She takes the readers on a chain around her neck

and sticks them on the end of her nose. Moving closer, she holds out a hand to finger the charm. "That's the Saint Nicholas bracelet, just like mine."

I check her wrists and feel a rush of excitement when I notice they're bare. "Could this be yours?"

She releases the gold medal and removes her glasses. "Mine is hanging on the tree." She points to the small fresh one in the corner, planted in a bucket. A match to those outside in pots flanking the entrance, it's trimmed with an assortment of antique glass ornaments and modern-day coffee-themed ones. "I hang it there during the week of Christmas."

"Are you sure it's here?" Sawyer asks.

"Of course." She walks toward the corner.

We follow. The coffee ornaments have white price tags dangling from their cords. She sells them every year and does a swift business from what I hear. People love their brew.

The pretty colors on the antiques are lovely. They must be from her personal collection. I bet Leo would love to get his hands on them.

Her arthritic fingers shift several branches aside and she looks the tree over. Her brow furrows and her fingers move more swiftly, going over the various decorations again. "Now where did I put it?"

After another scan, she becomes distressed, checking the inside of the pot and the floor around it. "It was just here, I swear. I got a new shipment of the Love You A Latte mug ornaments and I moved it..."

Her voice trails off and she stands back, hands on hips. "That's so weird. I can't believe I lost it."

Sawyer catches my eye. I hold out the bracelet again. "So this could be yours?"

She takes it from me, scrutinizing the clasp. "I wish it was now, but no, I'm afraid not. My fastener broke and I had to have it replaced three years ago. I've worn that bracelet nearly every day since I got it that Christmas when I was seven, and I guess I wore the thing out." She taps the catch on the one we brought. "This looks like an original."

I feel deflated once more. Sawyer finishes putting a chair on a table and smiles at her. "Well, thanks anyway. We'll let you get back to closing."

She follows us to the exit. "Almost time for the Jingle Bell Jam. I'm serving coffee at City Hall. You stop over if you get the chance." Her crooked fingers flip the lock. "I hope you find the owner."

I can see her distress over having lost hers. "I hope you locate yours, too."

Out on the street, Sawyer and I pause. "Cross that lead off," he says.

The last of the sinking sun splashes gold and pink across the sidewalk. Evening falls quickly this time of year. I think about checking in with Robyn, but she would have called if she had any leads. I'd love to hand her our list and let her do her detective thing, but she can't possibly interview every woman on it in the next two days in order to rule them out as suspects. Plus, she's not as certain as we are that the bracelet is even a clue.

As we stroll back to Enchanted, I consider dividing the names between my sisters. "Only four dozen more to go," I add.

While everyone wants to help, it's not fair to ask them to add another thing to their already overflowing to-do list.

"We may have to put up posters." Sawyer glances at his grandmother's shop window, already sporting the Christmas walk flyers. She's changing out one of the displayed quilts and waves at us. We return it. "We don't have to mention what type it is, or show a picture of it. Maybe we'll get a hit."

"Maybe." The Victorian street lamps come on, one by one, as the solar bulbs kick in. At the bookstore, Daisy is setting up a table outside with famous Christmas classics.

I replay what Betsy said in my head. "She could be lying. If she stole the angel and lost the bracelet, what better way to throw us off than to claim the clasp is different?"

"When did you become so skeptical?" He nudges me to let me know he's teasing, but I hear the truth under his words. He's right—I am. "What motive would she have for taking the angel?"

I have no idea. "It may not be obvious, but we can't rule her out completely."

"We've both known Betsy our whole lives. She wouldn't steal anything."

"She's getting up there in years. Maybe she's…I don't know…planning to sell it on eBay or something to help fund her retirement."

Sawyer laughs as if this is preposterous. "Or she just lost her bracelet. It does happen."

We pass Daisy and offer to assist her. She waves us off. "Belle will bop over in a minute and put the finishing touches on this. She's amazing, your sister." Daisy's smile is generous. She loves Belle like a mother. "This year's event is the best yet."

I agree, but I know the thefts will put a smudge on it for her. "Good luck tonight."

We stop outside Enchanted. "You know," Sawyer says, his tone filled with speculation, "it's possible our thief grabbed Betsy's to replace this." He taps my pocket where the bracelet is hidden.

It's true a lot of folks may have seen hers on the tree, including our culprit. "We're still back to square one. Who does it belong to, if not her?"

My sisters are frantically preparing for the Jingle Bell Jam. He says hello to them. Matilda and Uncle Odin are also helping with last minute decorations and restocking.

"Where have you two been?" Matilda asks.

Rissy is nowhere to be seen. "The Perking Pot," I tell her. "I was following up on a lead on who stole the angel."

Ruby passes me with a, "By the sound of your voice, you didn't find it."

"Nope." I pick up Rumpelstiltskin when he flies

into the room having heard me. He nestles under my chin and chitters. "A total bust."

"I should get out of your hair," Sawyer says to me.

"Running off so soon?"

Rissy appears from the back room. "You must be Sawyer." She struts across the floor, extending her hand. "I'm Rissy, Tilly's sister."

He looks slightly confused, but shakes it. "Nice to meet you. I didn't realize you had one," he says to Matilda.

"Yes," my godmother muses as she refills a stack of bags under the counter. "She's a surprise to all of us."

Rissy makes a noise in her throat and waves her hand through the air. "She's such a drama queen. Ignore her. Take your coat off and stay a while." She smiles up at him. "Tell me all about what you do."

He glances at me. "I can stay if you want. To help, I mean."

Cinder, passing by, stops and shoves three large candles into his arms. "We always need extra help. Put those over on that shelf, will you?"

He winks at me and does as instructed.

Rissy frowns and disappears again. Matilda works with a slight grin on her face, humming as she takes her position at the door to greet folks.

The downtown stores reopen at seven. Our shop looks beautiful when we once more welcome customers. Cinder decided to build a fire and the smell of the burning wood adds an extra layer of ambience.

Belle puts me at the register, with Sawyer next to me bagging purchases.

"You're sure Minerva doesn't need you?" I ask him, quickly braiding my growing hair.

"She has several volunteers from the quilt club hanging out to assist her."

I place Rumpel upstairs in my bedroom to keep him from being underfoot. We're forced to dive in right off the bat, the shop filling with holiday shoppers the moment Cinder flips the sign on the door.

The little girl from the tree lighting comes in with her brother. Belle greets them, and while she's speaking to the boy, Shelby makes her way to the counter. She stares at my hair and points to it. "It's just like the angel's."

I touch the plait and smile at her. "It is, isn't it?"

She glances around at the busy festivities and lowers her voice. "Are you an angel?"

When Sawyer snickers, I stomp on the top of his foot. He grimaces and turns away. "I'm afraid not," I tell her sincerely.

Shelby looks back at her mother, who's standing outside on the sidewalk talking to Uncle Odin. "Momma prays to them all the time. She put one above my bed, claiming it would protect me."

My breath stops. "Like the one from the wishing tree?"

"No. Mine is a baby angel holding a teddy bear."

I let out my breath. The wig she's wearing tonight, once again made from my strands, is a honey brown.

When I trim it, it retains the color it was at that time. I'm grateful it can help so many children who suffer from hair loss. "I'm sure you have many angels surrounding you."

She sneaks a letter out from inside her jacket and hands it to me. "Can you get this to Santa for me?" she whispers over the noise of the crowd.

Sawyer winks at her. "Absolutely." He takes it and slides it into a slot underneath the register. "This special portal will take it right to him."

Shelby grins wide. "I knew he lived here. Does he have to go up to the North Pole to check on the elves?"

Sawyer leans on the countertop, getting into the act. He lowers his voice as though he's about to tell her a secret. "It's a good thing he has magick, so he can get back and forth whenever he wants."

Delighted, Shelby grins at him, then at me. Her brother appears, taking her hand. "We need to get going," he says.

They're swallowed up by the crush of customers as they leave, and Sawyer and I are once again busy as Santa's elves.

Belle heads out to check on the downtown participants and make sure everything is running well. Two hours later, we close, and it takes another hour to clean up and restock. I'm dead on my feet, grateful that Sawyer stays to pitch in.

Belle returns looking as tired as I am and readies the bank deposit for the next morning. "Everyone I spoke with said tonight was a success."

"That's great," I tell her.

Cinder heads to the workroom to create more peppermint soap. Ruby takes Uncle Odin upstairs to get him a snack, and Matilda disappears into the turret, where I guess Rissy is now staying.

Once Belle goes in the office, it's just me and Sawyer. "Thank you for helping," I tell him. The whole time, it felt like the old us, working together, him teasing me, me threatening him. All done in good fun. I feel happier than I have in a long time.

"What do we do with that letter for Santa?" he asks.

"Since he's not real, we can't always predict what the parents are going to give the kids. We don't do anything with them."

"That's kind of Grinch-y."

I pull the letter out and open it. "Well, let's see what she asked for."

He sidles up to me and reads over my shoulder. Her printing is neat and flows evenly. She asks Santa how he is and then tells him the only thing she wants is for her brother to find his Christmas spirit once more. She mentions how he used to love the holidays, but now, because of her, he seems sad.

Sawyer's hand rests on my back. "It's got to be hard on both of them. He's probably worried that every Christmas is her last one."

Belle emerges, her phone ringing. She pulls it out of her apron pocket. "Hello?"

I look into Sawyer's eyes and my heart goes out to

Shelby's brother. According to the note, Cody is his name. "How do you give a kid back his Christmas spirit?"

Sawyer touches my hand holding the letter. "How do you give an adult back the same?"

Guilt surfaces. "Okay, okay, it's not your fault. Don't worry about it."

Belle comes to the counter, giving me a frantic look. "I'll be over in just a minute. Yes, he's here. I'll bring him with me."

The moment over, we turn to her. "What's going on?" Sawyer asks.

"That was your grandmother." Belle seems disturbed. "She was putting the Santa's Toy Sack box by the rear door to load in her car after closing. It was full and she intended to bring it to City Hall where we're storing them overnight so the volunteers can sort and deliver them on Christmas Eve. She went inside to grab her purse, and when she returned, it was gone."

I can't believe it. "The entire box?"

Belle nods wearily. "The whole thing."

Sawyer rubs his forehead. "Our thief?"

Tears brim in Belle's eyes. "Appears so."

She calls Cinder and Ruby in and tells them. Cinder insists on them helping us, but Belle says there's nothing for them to do. She, Sawyer, and I bundle up to go investigate.

As we stand by the door, Minerva goes on and on about how sorry she is. Belle puts her arm around the older woman's shoulder and tells her once again that it wasn't her fault.

"I should have been here to help you," Sawyer says.

"Don't be ridiculous," she scolds. "There was nothing you could do about it."

"I could have hauled it for you. Maybe this wouldn't have happened."

"Spilled milk," Belle says.

I scan the area and feel helpless. Sawyer walks the parking lot. Rumpel jumps from my arms and sniffs the ground.

"What is it?" I ask him.

Bending down, I study a track mark. "Sawyer, look at this." As he and the others draw close, I point to a skinny track. The mark goes all the way up to the back door where the box was sitting. "Could this be from a bike?"

"Possibly," he replies.

Belle frowns. "Must be a very small one. How could anyone carry a big box of toys on it?"

"Have you seen anyone hanging around here on a bike?" Sawyer asks Minerva.

She shakes her head. "Mr. Gleason rides his around town every morning, but he stays far away from me."

"Why is that?" Belle asks.

"Because she's been trying to set him up with Berna Tickler for years," Sawyer supplies.

Minerva rolls her eyes. "He needs a wife and she's a good cook."

Together, we straighten and follow the track from the shop, the faint marks disappearing in the alley that spans the entire block.

"An angel, a gingerbread house, and now a box of toys," I mutter to myself, taking out my phone to report this to Robyn. "What is our thief doing?"

Sawyer crosses his arms. "Looks like she's creating her own Christmas."

# SEVENTEEN

On Christmas Eve morning I wake to find Rissy in my room, sitting at my dressing table, playing with my collection of brushes. A mug of steaming liquid is next to her elbow.

"Excuse me," I say, sitting up. "What are you doing in here?"

The ferret has gathered my ribbons as though saving them from her and chitters at me from across the room where he's planted himself in the chair.

Rissy swivels away from the mirror and points to a file lying on the end of the bed. "Brought you something."

"In our family, we knock before entering some-one's room."

She winks. "Can you do my hair today?" She pivots back to face herself and runs her fingers through her dark locks. "I want it to look...not like Tilly's."

There is definitely something odd between these

two women. I'm curious to find out what, but... "I'm kinda busy."

She hands me the mug. "Too busy for family? I brought you coffee."

I accept it and notice it does appear untouched, so I take a sip. "You're not family, technically."

"Pfft." She makes a face. "I hear you're the absolute best hairstylist around."

"I am." The beverage is black the way I like it. I toe at the file. "What's in there?"

Hopping up, she tightens the belt of a kimono that belongs to Matilda, and reaches for it. "Your guy is clean. No debt, no affairs, no secret babies, and his credit score is over seven hundred. Better hang on to that one."

She hands me a sheet of paper and I gape at the information contained on it. "You ran a background check on Sawyer?"

"He's a unicorn. I'd snag him myself if he wasn't in love with you."

I stare at her in disbelief. "Has anyone ever talked to you about boundaries?"

She flaps a hand and returns to the makeup table, sorting through a drawer containing eyeshadows and blush. "Boundaries, schmoundaries. You're family, and I wanted to be sure he was good enough for you."

Wrapped in my own robe a minute later, I hunt down Matilda, the file in hand. She's in the kitchen with the others, the smell of cherry coffee cake filling the air.

Good mornings greet me and I nod in general as a response. Rumpel carries the ribbons in his mouth and hides them under the pie safe.

I slap the folder on the table next to Matilda's plate. "Your sister is out of line."

Her lids close for a heartbeat, then she opens them. "What did she do now?"

"She ran a background check on Sawyer, and she's currently in my room helping herself to my makeup."

Uncle Odin chuckles as he forks up a bite. "She's delightful, isn't she?"

I frown. "Matilda, what is going on with her? Why is she really here?"

Cinder sips coffee and stares at our godmother. Ruby removes her apron and sits, looking equally interested. Belle is the only one missing and I assume she's already running errands.

Matilda plays with her spoon, flipping it over and over. "The story is complicated and rather long."

"Give us the highlights," Cinder suggests.

She heaves a heavy sigh and glances at the three of us. "When I came here to care for you, my relatives disliked the idea. Valkyries are family oriented, but you aren't blood, you understand?"

We nod in unison and she continues. "Your mother was a friend when no one else was, and to me, you all are closer than my blood family. I'd do anything for you. Odin, too."

He smiles at her and continues eating.

"We're forever grateful that you came," Ruby says. "We think of you as family."

"Mine disowned me for this choice, and Rissy believes I abandoned her in favor of you. She's right. I left her behind and it wasn't easy for her."

Cinder sits back in her chair. "I'm sorry we came between you."

"Not your fault." She releases the spoon, putting her hands in her lap. "It was my decision and I don't regret it."

"So she's here to make up with you?" I ask.

"Yes and no." She glances at the file. "Her last mission went a little sideways and her employer suggested she take a long vacation. Returning home with her tail between her legs isn't her style—she doesn't want anyone to know she's been disciplined. So, she found me, knowing I'd never turn her away or pass judgment on her."

"Mission?" I query. "What exactly is her job?"

Matilda stares at the table. "She's a spy."

For the second time that morning, I gape. "A what? For who?"

"Interpol." She points at the background check. "She was trying to be helpful, is all. It's what she does —she's suspicious of everyone and everything. Checking Sawyer's records is standard protocol for her."

Cinder, Ruby, and I exchange a glance. "Well," Cinder says, "that's not what I expected."

Uncle Odin points at the cooling cake. "Could you pass that, please?"

Still dumbfounded, I do. "We have a spy under our roof."

"She's quite good," Matilda assures us. "This last incident sounds like it wasn't really her fault."

An idea strikes, and I turn on my heel, gathering the file. Matilda calls after me, but I ignore her, finding Rissy still in my room, applying a deep red lipstick to her lips. "What do you think?"

I brandish the folder. "Can you run checks on anyone?"

She makes kissy lips at herself in the mirror. "Sure. Why?"

"Does it take long?"

A shrug. "Depends, but usually not."

"Is it unethical, immoral, or illegal?"

She grins. "Not if you do it right."

I narrow my eyes, considering the idea.

"It's not illegal to run one," she assures me, "but even if it was, I can—"

I hold up a hand to stop her. "I don't want to know, okay?"

"I didn't mean to upset you. I was simply looking out for your best interests. I wanted to be sure he wasn't a crook or a philanderer."

Rummaging through my things, I pull out the list of names I wrote down yesterday. Before bed, I put stars by three people of dubious reputation who seemed like potential candidates for our thief. I'd planned to take them to Robyn, but asking Rissy to run them might not be a bad idea either. "Can you see what turns up on those marked with a star?"

Scanning the names as I hold the paper, she nods. "Is this about that thief you're all up in arms over?" She shoots to her feet. "I'll have a report to you in an hour. Will that be soon enough?"

An image of Lovey climbing into my chair at the salon stops me. I think about Betsy's arthritis. Pulling the list back, I pause. The women on it are all aged, and even someone like Nonni, who's in good health, would have a terrible time climbing a boom or carrying off a large gingerbread house or box of toys.

"Never mind," I tell Rissy. "The culprit isn't on here."

"How do you know?" She seems almost eager to grab the sheet away from me. "The best thieves are the ones you never suspect."

I think about Shelby. She's only six and definitely not the woman from the video stealing the angel. Her mother, though...

"Megan Larins." I spell it out for her. "See what you can dig up on her, will you?"

She writes it down. "You'll do my hair for Christmas?"

I shake her outstretched hand. "It will be a piece of art by the time I finish."

CHAPTER

# EIGHTEEN

After a quick shower, I head to the tower and sit in Eunice's chair, combing through my favorite spellbook. Rumpelstiltskin follows, staying close as if to protect me from Rissy.

In the fall, Snow used an intention spell to make sure Broden was a good man to hire for her farm. I need a similar one to show me Sawyer's true feelings.

According to my grandmother's journals, she created a lot of love spells and sold them covertly. As I thumb through her collection, I find several "recipes" with her handwritten notes in the margins. It takes forever, however, for me to find a potion that meets my needs. I find *Determining a Soulmate* and skim the directions quickly. This might be it.

Carrying the book downstairs to the shop kitchen, I hurriedly begin gathering supplies. There are two ingredients I have to substitute, and I hope they won't cause it to misfire. Trying to hunt them down the day before Christmas is out of the question.

A few minutes before opening, Belle brings me a mug of eggnog, Jayne following at her feet. "Robyn called to say no luck with anyone she's questioned from last night."

"I'm sorry." I don't try to hide what I'm doing because I'm in a hurry, and well, she's my twin. She'll figure it out anyway. "I still have a lead that I'm following up on."

"I appreciate what you and Sawyer have done." She leans over to read the title of the recipe. "Ah, is this what you've been mixing up all week? Potions for true love?"

"No. Some of them have been to keep heartbreak away, and I really have been experimenting with hair conditioners." I don't look at her as I stir. "But I need to know how Sawyer feels about me, and I found this."

She leans against the counter, sipping her own drink. Jayne and Rumpelstiltskin play with a ball between the two of them. "I'm sure he still has feelings for you. It's obvious you do for him as well. You wouldn't get so defensive and upset if you didn't."

I drop one of Sawyer's hairs from his trim into the bubbling liquid. "I want to let it go," I confess. "It's just not that easy."

She leans over to look at the potion, screwing up her nose at the smell. "Is this one of Eunice's?"

The odor makes me back away for a moment as

well. "If the person in question is my soulmate, the liquid will turn red. If not? It stays a dull gray."

"And if it turns green?"

Sure enough, when I hold my breath and peer over the edge, the bubbling liquid is a shade of lime. "No idea." I sigh. "I didn't have the exact ingredients so I tried to use some that are close. It's probably a toss-up now."

She pats my shoulder. "You don't need a potion to tell you if he's your soulmate. Your heart knows."

The dog and ferret get into a quarrel over the toy and she goes to break it up. I dump the potion down the sink and begin washing the cauldron.

When she returns, she offers to dry it, so I hand it to her. "I wonder what our thief will steal tonight. The chamber will never put me in charge of another event again."

I wipe my hands on a towel and feel her fear circulating between us. "Wait! I could try a spell to reveal their identity." I wonder why I didn't think of it before. "There has to be one."

Belle looks excited. "I haven't seen any, but I bet you're right. Do you have time to research it for me?"

Without spending hours going through Eunice's books, I don't. Luckily, there's always the internet. I pull out my phone and do a search, coming across one that only requires three ingredients. "This should do."

As Belle goes to open the store, I gather the supplies and light the candle as instructed. This isn't a potion to make in the cauldron, but rather a divination technique, like reading runes or tarot cards. It can't identify the person exactly, but it can send me in the right direction, if I ask the proper questions.

I haven't done a spell like this in a long time, and no matter what I ask or how I phrase it, I get no confirmation. I even pull out a pendulum and begin asking more specifically about certain people, including Megan. All the crystal does is tremble at the end of the chain, indicating there isn't enough information.

While I'm working, my hair goes silver. For a moment, I wonder if my magick is wonky and that's why I'm not getting answers.

Giving up on finding our thief's identity, I focus on changing my hair color to a more festive holiday shade of red. It seems to work until I'm walking to the salon for my first appointment and see Sawyer on his motorcycle leaving the quilt shop. Instantly, my hair turns the same color green as the earlier potion.

I hustle into the salon and stare at it in horror. While I generally like the color lime, it makes me look sick. I try to get my emotions under control and wonder what the meaning is.

As I'm focusing, my heart and pulse seem to be racing. It's Christmas Eve, when I normally feel depressed and sad. Today I feel...anticipation.

When I check my hair, the cranberry red is back. I heave a sigh of relief. It's down past my shoulders and I braid it to keep it out of the way. My first client arrives, so I get her into the chair, thankful to have something to take my mind off Sawyer and my sister's anxiety about tonight.

Matilda and Rissy drop in shortly after lunchtime. Matilda is dressed in a gorgeous velvet Christmas skirt and top. She's wearing her usual assortment of extravagant jewelry; she also has the cutest purple boots on her feet.

"Are those mine?" I ask, even though I know they are.

Rissy beams. "I picked them."

Matilda looks down and wiggles her toes. "They go perfect with my outfit, don't you think?"

"Honestly, no. I would have chosen brown or black."

She knows this is a lie and grins.

Rissy does as well. "They were buried in the back of your closet. I thought somebody should put them to good use. Boots make the woman, you know. They can open doors for you."

The sisters seem to be getting along better, so I decide to let it go and change the subject. I glance around, but no one's paying any attention. I think half the women here are afraid of Matilda; the others are in awe. I lower my voice anyway. "Did anything come up on that...subject...I asked you to look into?"

Rissy picks up a brush and twirls it. "Nothing out of the ordinary. Debt, debt, and more debt. The house she lives in belonged to her parents. Husband left her five years ago." She sets it down. "Boring."

Matilda frowns between us. "Who?"

Disappointment seeps into my bones. I didn't want it to be her, but that was my best lead. "No one. What are two doing today?"

Matilda plops into my chair and looks at herself in the mirror, whisking a lock from her face. "I need something new, sexy."

My next appointment is in thirty minutes. Rissy will want to cash in our deal, too. "Do you want something with a holiday theme?"

Her snowman earrings jangle as she nods. "Of course. I want to look angelic, you know, like your natural color, and it wouldn't hurt if it makes me appear ten years younger."

I meet her gaze. "That may take more magick than I'm capable of."

She swivels the chair and smacks me on the backside as Rissy snorts. I jump out of her reach and head for the supply room to mix up the colors.

Since it's my godmother and her sister, I do use a bit of beauty magick to speed up the coloring process on Matilda and the style Rissy wants. Like Edward Scissorhands, I make each design unique and dramatic before they leave my chair.

At four, I'm cleaning up. The salon is closing early, and all of us have to get to the play. I'm the last to leave, since I've been at the arboretum styling Anna and the others for the wedding, but before I can lock up, Shelby's mother arrives.

Megan gives me a little wave as she stands just inside the doorway. She's bundled in a worn wool coat that hangs to her knees, and her shoes are tattered. "I'm sorry if this is a bad time. I just thought it might be nice to get a trim for Christmas."

If I'm going to get Uncle Odin ready for the play, I need to get back to Enchanted now. The thought of turning her away, however, doesn't even enter my mind. I motion her over and grab a clean cape to put around her neck. "I'm glad you took me up on the offer. How much were you thinking of taking off?"

Fifteen minutes later, I have her smiling at her reflection. As she slides out of the seat, turning her head this way and that, her new do bounces around her shoulders. She gives a little giggle. "I can't believe how getting my hair styled can make me feel so much lighter."

While this woman certainly deserves some magick in her life, I didn't even have to use any on her. A simple cut and style did the trick. This is one of the reasons I love my job. I hand her a sample bottle of conditioner. "This will keep the fly-aways to a minimum. Oh, and I have something else for you, too."

From my purse, I bring out a blue glass bottle. "This is a serum I've been working on. All organic, and it nourishes the hair follicles. Have your daughter rub a drop or two in her scalp about an hour before bed every night. It will stimulate hair growth."

Tears well in her eyes. "Thank you," she says, accepting it.

On the off chance she might know something about the bracelet, I pull it from my apron pocket. "I know this is an odd question, but have you ever seen this before?"

Her dark eyes widen before she glances away. She digs in her purse for her car keys. "Can't say I have. Is it yours?"

"No, I'm trying to find the owner. She lost it the other night at the tree lighting. I'm sure she's missing it."

"Good luck with that." She doesn't look at me as she opens the glass door to leave. "Thank you again, and Merry Christmas."

I stand and watch as she exits the parking spot, suspicion about her once more tightening my chest.

CHAPTER

# NINETEEN

The stars are out, shining brightly overhead. My breath frosts in the air creating plumes in front of me, as I hustle Uncle Odin to the makeup table behind the stage and rapidly apply rouge to his cheeks, and liner around his eyes.

The actors are warming up, reciting lines quietly as the audience files around the grounds. Sawyer is busy checking the lights and sound equipment. We passed each other briefly when Uncle Odin and I arrived, but I didn't have time to tell him everything I'd learned. I did share that I suspect our thief is not in the age bracket with our grandmothers.

I ensure no one's watching, I call on my magick. Waving my hands over my uncle's white hair and beard, I add length and volume to each.

"Oh my," he says, his voice full of wonder. "You are so talented."

I've added six inches to his beard, and his mane is

now long enough to hang over his shoulders, like mine currently is. The ends are curling here and there.

His eyes twinkle in the small square mirror in front of him. "Very good, Zelle. I rather like this look."

"Hey, Zelle?"

Startled, I whirl to find Robyn and Rainhart pushing past a curtain to get to us. Thankfully, even if they did witness my spell, neither is shocked by it.

"We were in the neighborhood," Robyn says, her smile self-conscious as she glances at Rain. "I wanted to update you."

I comb through Uncle Odin's beard and add a few thin silver strands to make it sparkle on stage. We're five minutes from the curtain rising. "Belle already told me. You haven't had any luck."

"Actually, I'm looking into Cody Watson's parents." She peeks over her shoulder to make sure no one is eavesdropping. "It's a long shot, but one of the ladies who attended the contest last night claims she saw Cody's father put a large object under a blanket on his son's lap before he wheeled him away. She didn't think much about it at the time, figuring maybe someone had given the kid a gift or something. I've left messages and went by their house, but there's been no answer. I'm hoping they attend the play tonight."

That certainly seems suspicious. Fiddling with my braid, I debate whether or not to mention Megan's reaction to the bracelet. "Do you really think the Watsons are behind all of this?"

"John and Bethany have good jobs," Rain offers.

"They don't have lots of cash to throw around, but they don't seem poor either."

I think about the tire track behind Minerva's shop. "Could that track we found be from a wheelchair?"

Robyn nods. "I wondered that, too. I don't have enough for a warrant to get an impression made from Cody's to see if it matches. I need something more concrete in order to check."

"Three minutes," Belle calls out. Sawyer blinks the lights to let the noisy audience out front know it's time to take their seats.

"We better go," Rain says, taking Robyn's hand.

She lets him and I see a blush steal across her cheeks. "Let's regroup afterward," she tells me.

"You two should come by the house tonight for cookies and eggnog," Uncle Odin tells her. "We'd love to have you."

She leans over and pecks his cheek. "We'll do that."

When everything is underway, I pull Sawyer aside to tell him about Megan. He keeps an eye on the actors so he doesn't miss his cues with the curtains. Finn is nearby running the lights. "We can't prove it's hers," he whispers, "just because she seemed nervous about it."

I'm so close to him, I can smell the soap and shampoo he used earlier. My heart does a funny pitter-patter and I notice my hair is starting to shimmer. The silver turns pink, then yellow.

*Oh no. Not now.*

I close my eyes and insist my magick stabilize. When I open them, Sawyer is looking at me funny. "Everything okay?"

"Fine," I say under my breath.

I force myself not to stare at him or think about what his whispered voice does to me. I think about Shelby's letter to Santa. How her brother needed his holiday spirit back. "It makes sense Megan's behind it. Robyn believes it was a woman who stole the angel, and Megan doesn't have any money for toys. She may not even have enough for food. One guess who's trying to build their own Christmas."

The first scene ends and Finn lowers the lights. Sawyer hauls on the pulleys to close the large burgundy curtains. The actors hustle backstage, and Uncle Odin gives me thumbs up as he passes. "Let's talk later," I say to Sawyer. "Robyn has a different suspect, but I think I should tell her my theory."

During the next scene, I step out the back of the amphitheater, making my way around to look at the audience. Lawn chairs have been set up, and I see many familiar faces, including Sawyer's grandma and most of my family. Others are on blankets, sharing hot cocoa from Betsy's booth, and cider from Snow's.

As I scan the crowd, I notice Shelby is in the audience with a woman who must be her aunt. While I was trimming Megan's hair, she mentioned Shelby and Connor were spending a few hours with Corine, making homemade Christmas gifts.

Matilda waves at me from her place on the far

right, Rissy and Cinder next to her. Her angelic hair seems to sparkle in the moonlight and I'm glad my magick can make her happy, even though mine has started doing the rainbow effect again. I wrap my braid as best as I can in a bun and snug up my hood so no one can see it.

As the kids cheer for Santa at the end of the second act, Megan arrives. She gets her sister's attention and Corine follows her to the parking lot several yards away.

I pretend not to pay attention, and I can't eavesdrop, as the audience is chatting too loudly, but I slowly work my way closer to them. Matilda and Rissy join me, and Rissy sends her gaze toward the sisters who appear to be arguing. "Is that her?"

"The one with the bob," I confirm. "That's Megan, my suspect. Problem is, I have no proof."

"What are you two up to?" Matilda asks, following our gazes.

I turn both of them around to face me, so the other women don't realize what I'm up to. "Act normal. Don't stare."

People are lining up at Betsy and Snow's booths. Belle jumps in to help her so everyone can get seated again for the third and final act.

I smile at the sisters, pretending we're discussing something else. "I think I know who our thief might be, but don't tell anyone yet."

Both nod and smile back. Just a plain ol' normal

conversations. "Do you want me to get closer to see if I can get the goods on them?" Rissy asks.

Goddess be. That's the last thing I need her to do. "No. No stalking. I could very well be wrong and it's Christmas Eve. The last thing Megan needs is to be wrongly accused if she's not behind all of this."

From her seat, Shelby has twisted around to watch her mother and aunt as well. Megan motions at her, and I see her longingly glance between her and the stage, realizing her mom is about to take her away.

When she doesn't immediately join them, Megan calls her name. "Shelby Larins! We have to go!"

The girl's disappointment is palpable across the lawn. Slowly she gets to her feet and drags them across the distance until she's three feet from her mother. Megan steps forward, grabs her hand, and hustles her to the car.

"Let her stay," Corine says loud enough for me to hear. "It's not her fault."

Megan looks as if she's ready to burst a blood vessel. "You should have stayed out of this."

The stage lights flicker; the third act is about to start. The audience hustles to their chairs, and I motion for Matilda and Rissy to go back to theirs.

"You're sure?" Rissy asks. "I could follow her."

"In what?" Matilda counters. "We walked. You don't have a vehicle."

"No stalking," I remind them as I watch Megan and Shelby drive away. "Go enjoy the play, and I'll see you both at home."

Matilda grabs Rissy's arm and tugs her toward their seats. Rissy glances at me over her shoulder and I smile, signaling as though I'm going to watch the end from here.

Everyone is settled in, and the final act begins. I consider my options of staying or finding the evidence Robyn needs.

The curtain rises. From the corner of my eye, I see Corine staring after Megan's car. Then she shakes her head, gets in her own, and peels out.

I pull my hood tighter about my face and follow.

# TWENTY

Megan, Shelby, and Corine are long gone by the time I get to the street. I head for Enchanted, using my phone to look up the Larins' address.

Once there, I find the keys to the van. Rumpelstiltskin insists on going with me and I bring one of Savannah's cat beds for him to snuggle in on the passenger seat.

Sawyer texts me to ask where I went, and I explain I'm checking on the Larins. I don't share what I overheard, but he knows me. He tells me he'll meet me at their place and not to do anything foolish.

As if that would stop me.

All I want to do is snoop a bit and see if I can find the stolen goods, then I'll call Robyn. I wish I had time to refine that spell but my gut tells me I don't need magick to suss out our thief now.

The rundown house is located south of town off

the county highway. As I steer onto the gravel road leading to it, the van bounces in and out of potholes and Rumpelstiltskin climbs into my lap, not liking the rough treatment. Above me, the stars shine brightly, and I need to turn up the heat. The walk to the shop allowed the cold weather to seep into my bones and I'm chilled.

What will I say to Megan if she's the one who's stolen the assorted items? How will I handle confronting her in front of her kids?

I won't, I decide, apologizing to the ferret when another rut makes me slide sideways. Cinder will hex me if I wreck the drive shaft or blow a tire. "If I discover any proof, I'll call Robyn and let her handle it," I tell Rumpelstiltskin.

Although even that makes my stomach clench. What will happen to the children? I can't stand the idea of Shelby and her brother ending up in state care or a foster home. I wish with all my might I could put a ribbon on the angel tree and ask for a happy resolution.

My familiar places his paws on the steering wheel as if assisting my driving technique and peers over the top. The headlights bounce off the rocky path. "Maybe it's not her," I say out loud, warming to the idea. "Tell me I've missed the mark, Rumpel."

He chitters, but it doesn't convince me. Set back on the acreage, the farmhouse is barely visible amongst an assortment of rusted out vehicles, and rundown buildings surrounding it. I ease off the road and park in between an abandoned shed with one metal wall partially missing and a tangle of overgrown brush. My anxiety spikes at what I'm about to do, what could happen to this family.

Breathing in through my nose and exhaling through my mouth, I count the number of oak trees I can make out on the property. Then I stroke the ferret's fur and count to one hundred. I consider what color to change my hair to for New Year's Eve, and wonder if Anna's wedding went okay.

From town gossip, I know Megan's husband left shortly after Shelby's diagnosis. She's been hit with one thing after another. All the more reason I feel guilty trying to prove she did this. I'd do anything for my sisters, even commit a crime, if I were in a similar predicament.

Approaching without being spotted is a slow process. Sleet-like rain begins to fall, making the ground slippery. There doesn't appear to be any guard dog, which is a relief, and Rumpelstiltskin peeks out from the front of my coat to chitter at me. I dare not put him down, dog or no, for fear he'll give away our presence. "Shh, little one," I whisper. "We must be as quiet as the stars, okay?"

Those overhead twinkle sharp and clear, the night air sinking deep into my bones. The sleet sticks on my wool jacket in tiny balls, and I slip through a busted piece of fence that used to corral horses back when this property was owned my Megan's grandparents. Edging closer to the house, I crouch by a crumbling well that hasn't been used in decades. A bush has grown up and over it. From here, I can see there's a single light on downstairs.

For the next few minutes, I stay put, listening to nocturnal animals and shivering. An owl perches on the high branch of a pine tree, keeping an eye on me. Rumpel tries to climb out of my coat and run off, so I point to our audience. "You don't want to be dinner for that one."

Seeming to understand, he finally nestles down in an interior pocket, curling into a ball. The owl cocks his head and wings off slowly, his dinner plans averted.

The sleet begins to fall harder now, so I say a spell under my breath, allowing my already long hair to grow fuller. I shake it out from under the hood and it wraps around me and the ferret, adding a layer of insulation.

A soft light comes on upstairs and I see Shelby step to the window. I suspect it's her bedroom, and without a wig, I notice a layer of fuzz on her head. Her hair is starting to grow back—I hope my serum will help it.

Her pale face turns to look up at the sky, now dotted with low lying clouds. Sleet pings against the glass, but she studies the sky with rapt attention. I remember being a kid on Christmas Eve, doing the same, waiting and watching for Santa and his reindeer.

I'm about to edge closer to see if I can look in the

downstairs window when a squeaking noise to my left draws my attention. Connor comes into view, pulling a small red wagon behind him down a narrow horse trail I couldn't see in the dark. It must be a way for him to get to town and back, avoiding the county road.

Shelby doesn't seem to notice, her attention still on the sky. I crouch lower, my knees protesting over holding the position so long in the cold, and ease deeper into the bush to make sure Connor doesn't notice me. As he draws near, I realize he has a small, decorated tree in the wagon. It wobbles as he goes over the uneven ground, falling sideways and nearly toppling out. He stops, only a few feet from me, to straighten it, and I hold my breath.

My memory sparks—I'm sure I've seen that tree before. It's a clone to those outside Betsy's coffee shop.

What is he doing this time of night, walking from here to town? Connor pulls the wagon into the woods behind the house and the squeaking sounds fade. Where is he going?

Torn between following him and sneaking up to the house to peek in a window, I straighten but stay put. Could Connor be our thief?

The thought makes my stomach roll even harder. His height could be mistaken for a woman, his wagon could've left the track behind Minerva's shop. Things are starting to add up.

A car flies up the long driveway before I can follow him. Corine exits it and briskly hustles into the house, head down against the ice pellets. She doesn't knock, simply enters, and as I pick my way across the lawn, I get close enough to hear her and Megan arguing.

Listening intently, I still can't make out what they're saying. They seem to be following each other through different rooms on the first floor and all I can understand is the heat level of the disagreement.

Poor Shelby, I think, hearing all that on Christmas Eve.

The owl swoops close overhead, checking for the ferret. I duck and when he doesn't see the little guy, the bird turns for the woods. I gather my hair and wind it around my waist. With Rumpel's warm body curled next to mine, I decide to follow Connor.

Tramping through the woods, I wonder if I've lost my mind. Fog has begun to rise and floats in and around the trees. I wish I was back at Enchanted with a cup of something warm in my hands, the Christmas Eve festivities ready to begin. I also wonder where Sawyer is.

I see the red wagon up ahead, parked next to a camper near the river. Normally, the rapid water would be easy to hear, but the woods are thick in this area, and it has slowed due to the time of year. Come spring, it will race again and overflow its banks.

Connor emerges from the camper and grabs hold of the tree, hauling it up the three steps to take it inside. With all quiet, I carefully pick my way over and find an old cooler near the rear of the vehicle. I prop it under one of the windows.

Boosting myself up, I'm able to peek through a lace

curtain and see the decorated tree is on a table. My breath catches—on the top is the stolen angel.

Connor! It's been him, not his mom, all along.

He places gifts around the bottom, and I have no doubt they came from the toy drive.

"He's just a kid."

The woman's voice startles me. I jump, nearly falling as I pivot at the same time. Corine eyes me from a few feet away.

"All he wants is for his sister to have the Christmas of her dreams. She may not make it to the next one."

My heart goes out to all of them. "I understand that, and I'm very sorry things aren't better for your family, but the items Connor has taken belong to other people. The angel is owned by the town. Some kids won't have much if the toy drive doesn't provide a present."

She steps toward me, her shadowed features set in hard lines. "You're not taking those away from us."

I step off the cooler. "My sisters and I can help you. We can get a tree and gifts for the kids."

She laughs without humor, the sound sharp in the night air. "Oh heaven forbid—my sister—*stepsister*, I should clarify—won't accept charity." The words are said with scorn and tired disappointment.

"It's not charity. It's community. We take care of our own in Story Cove. You've all been through a lot. Everyone will understand about Connor and the stolen items."

For a moment, Corine looks as if she's going to nod

and accept my help. But then, she takes her hand out of her coat pocket and light from the camper glints off metal. "As I said, you're not going to take them. You're right, we have been through a lot, and none of it is Shelby or Connors's fault."

Tiny ice pellets catch on my lashes and I blink them away, staring at the gun pointed at me. My hair comes loose from my waist and Rumpelstiltskin pops his head out, fear racing through his body and making it quiver.

As my extremely long locks flow around me, the rainbow of colors starts up. Corine takes a step back, her eyes wide as she watches it unfurl in waves around me. It looks and acts like a shield. Matilda would be happy, I bet.

Rumpel leaps from my pocket and Corine startles, aiming at him.

"Don't you dare," I shout.

A squeak comes from behind me, and Connor appears on the porch. "Aunt Corine? What are you doing?"

"Go back in the camper," she insists, her attention on my crazy hair. "As soon as I'm done taking care of this woman, I'll go get Shelby."

Connor glances between us, his eyes lingering for a heartbeat on my strands and then stopping on the gun. "She's nice, Aunt Corine. Don't hurt her, okay? Shelby really likes her."

This is about to go all kinds of wrong. "I promise I won't say anything to anyone," I tell her. "I'll figure out something so you and your family have a great Christmas. We'll talk about helping you after the holidays."

"Get inside, Connor." She's still staring at my hair, which continues to flow around me. Connor watches it, too, now, but with fascination rather than horror.

Our eyes meet through the tresses. I nod at him with a forced smile. "It's going to be okay. Do as your aunt says."

As he reluctantly steps in and shuts the door behind him, Corine cocks the gun. "Start walking."

Rumpelstiltskin rushes toward her, making her jump back with a suppressed squeak. At the same moment, Sawyer steps out from behind a tree, tackling her.

He wrestles the weapon from her, her movements sending her sprawling. Once he's secured it, he ignores her kicks at his legs and sets her on her feet. "What in the world are you doing?"

I can't tell if he's talking to her or me. Corine takes one look between the two of us, pivots on her heel, and races off.

Magick pours through me, my hair suddenly becoming a lasso. Lightning fast, it snakes out and wraps around her ankles. I give it a jerk and she belly flops to the ground.

She lands hard, knocking the air from her lungs. "I'm sorry." Both she and Sawyer stare at me and my lasso in disbelief. "This is not how I wanted this to end."

Robyn and Megan come into sight, and Robyn pulls out her handcuffs. "Nice work, Zelle," she says to me, tugging Corine up.

The woman snarls at her stepsister. "This is all your fault!"

Megan looks sad yet resolute, "I don't take charity, but I also don't steal from good folks."

Sawyer hands the gun to Robyn, who puts it in an evidence bag. Rain comes running in from the path. "This is the most exciting Christmas I've ever had!"

Robyn glares at him. "I told you to stay in the squad car."

"I wanted to see my girlfriend in action!"

She rolls her eyes. "Santa save us."

As she marches the woman toward the house and the waiting cruiser, Matilda and Rissy rush to me.

"Are you okay?" My godmother hugs me then looks at all my hair, trailing on the ground. It's gone back to its silver coloring and seems to glow in the darkness around us. "You're lighting up the night."

I scoop up Rumpel and set him inside my coat. "I'm fine, although I need a trim."

Rissy laughs. "Have you ever thought about becoming a detective?"

I scoff. "I'll leave this stuff to you and Robyn."

Sawyer laughs, putting an arm around my shoulders. "You done good, Rebel."

Megan apologizes profusely. "I'm just so, so sorry. I never thought she'd do anything like this. Connor may have taken that tree, but she stole the angel and the other things. You've been so kind to me and my kids, I can only imagine what you think about us now."

I tell her not to worry, that everything is going to be okay.

As her son steps out, a sad expression on his face as he hears her words, I hope I can keep that promise.

# TWENTY-ONE

I refuse to press charges against Corine, but she broke several laws and Robyn has to hold her accountable for those.

Megan insists on returning the items, so even though it's late, she, Connor, and Shelby become their own version of Santa. We all watch as Connor helps Belle place the angel on the town tree.

My hair is at least cooperating at the moment, its natural color shining through. Sawyer keeps me close to him, and I let him hold my hand.

As we watch the angel regain her rightful place, I feel another hand in mine, looking down to find Shelby staring up at me. "Thank you for letting Aunt Corine off the hook. I don't think Momma's going to be as forgiving."

I tug the girl near and give her a hug. "Miracles happen at Christmas. You never know."

Her intense eyes drill into mine. She's once more

wearing one of my wigs. "Your hair looks just like mine. Can we be twins?"

Connor sidles over and puts his hand on her shoulder, as I smile and give her another squeeze. "Absolutely. You can never have too many sisters, just ask Belle."

"I'm really sorry, Miss Zelle," Connor tells me.

His mother joins us. "We both are. We're grateful for everything you've done for us."

As I rise, I offer her an embrace as well. "That's what family is about, community, Christmas. We're all in this together."

We go with them to return the tree to the coffee shop. Betsy is inside cleaning up from the play and she opens when we knock. "Why, there's my tree. I wondered where it went."

Connor apologizes, and Megan explains the whole story. Betsy nods, smiles, and tells them to keep it, that she has plenty. She also makes sure I know that she found her lost bracelet. "It fell behind my tree," she says pointing at the corner, "and was tangled in the skirt."

"That reminds me," Megan says after we bid Betsy a Merry Christmas and leave. "That bracelet you found?"

I pull it from my pocket. "It is yours?"

Shelby stands in front of her and Megan puts her hands on the girl's frail shoulders. "It belonged to my grandmother. Corine stole it from me years ago when our parents married. I wasn't sure that was it when you showed it to me, but today when I searched Corine's jewelry box, where she always kept it, I saw it was missing."

I hand it to her. "Well, I'm happy to return it."

She gives it to Shelby. "You should have this. Grandmama would want you to."

Shelby holds it up to examine the medal. "Is it Jesus?" the little girl asks, staring at the saint.

"No, but close," her mother assures her. "They both bless us with miracles."

Uncle Odin, in his Santa suit, Matilda, and Rissy pile into the van with us to deliver toys to Belle's list of a dozen local kids. Sawyer drives, and although it takes some time, it's worth seeing the joy on the faces of every one of the families we visit.

Our last stop is to return the gingerbread house to Adele, a little worse for wear, but still beautiful. When Megan, Shelby, and Connor stand on her doorstep to express their regret, she does the same as Betsy and tells them to keep it if they want. She even goes into her kitchen and comes back with a basket filled with bread, jam, and other treats for Christmas morning.

Once our mission is complete, we invite them over for hot cocoa. While the kids play with our pets and enjoy Ruby's candies, I send Sawyer, Rissy, and Matilda back to Megan's home to leave a few of the toys I withheld from the stack on the doorstep.

Robyn and Rain arrive, bringing a glass ornament for the tree and a Yule log cake that Rain's aunt made.

They join us in singing a few Christmas carols and I make everyone gather in front of the tree for pictures.

Poor Shelby nearly falls asleep afterward, curled up with Jayne and Rumpelstiltskin. "Guess we better get her home," Megan says.

I hug her and we make plans to meet up again soon. Shelby, fighting a yawn, tugs me aside and motions for me to bend down so she can whisper in my ear, her eyes tracking Uncle Odin as he rocks Savannah in his lap. "Is Santa going to put coal in my stocking because of what happened?"

"Never," I assure her. "You and Connor will have plenty of gifts to open in the morning."

Once they leave, Cinder stokes up a fire, Ruby puts my Christmas playlist on the speaker system, and Matilda and Rissy look smug. "We snuck in the house to hide the presents for Shelby and Connor," Matilda tells me. "I left Megan a note that they're in her closet. That way she can play Santa tonight."

"You broke in?"

She points at her sister. "She did it."

Rissy gives me a *what's the big deal* look. "Stop worrying. She'll thank us tomorrow."

Minerva arrives at the same time Nonni and Poppi do. "Ah, you're here," she says to Nonni, shrugging off her coat and taking an envelope from her pocket. "Guess what? After I tallied all the votes, you won the contest!"

Nonni puts a hand to her chest. "You're kidding!"

We all clap and laugh as she accepts the prize and

beams—a gift card to the quilt shop. "I can't believe it."

Uncle Odin and Matilda sneak off and return a few minutes later, arms loaded with gifts.

As Sawyer and Minerva gather around the tree with us, I notice there are several presents for them as well. Finn and Leo join us and we bring all the chairs from other rooms to gather near the fireplace.

On Christmas Eve, it's tradition in our family to open one gift apiece. As I watch my family enjoy this preview for the next day, I find myself leaning into Sawyer's shoulder.

Rumpelstiltskin makes a bed in his lap, and Sawyer kisses my temple. "Please, don't ever scare me like that again," he murmurs in my ear. "You took ten years off my life."

I squeeze his hand. "That seems about even for the four years you wasted by not being here with me."

"Are we ever going to get past that?"

Matilda, who's been eavesdropping, pats his leg as she hands out eggnog. "She may forgive you, but she'll never forget. You're going to be making it up to her for the rest of your lives."

Sawyer grins and Matilda winks at me as I accept the beverage. "But that means you have to stay," I tell him. "for the rest of yours."

His grandmother pokes him in his side. "I second that."

"Guess it's settled then," he says. "I'm here for good."

# TWENTY-TWO

I wake on Christmas filled with good cheer for the first time in many years. My family is gathered in the kitchen, and we share a hearty breakfast before we go downstairs to the tree. Belle gets the honor of handing out gifts this year, and soon we all have a stack beside us.

My sisters love their presents from me, Ruby's business cards being the biggest hit, but the money for the building fund and the bonus cash I give to Belle for her bookstore dream are solid wins, too.

Matilda gives Rissy a small box. Inside is a brooch. "If you'd warned me you were coming, I would've had something more for you."

"Any of those earrings or bracelets you've made would have been enough." She holds it up and studies it. "This was mother's, wasn't it?" When Matilda nods, Rissy's eyes tear up. "It's perfect. Thank you."

She offers her sister a festive bag. From inside,

Matilda pulls out a pair of boots—purple with a warm wool lining and buckles down the sides. Rissy winks at me. "Now you don't have to borrow Zelle's."

We shower Uncle Odin with small handmade gifts and receive the same from him. He's carved a miniature wooden Santa for all of us and Cinder lines them up on the mantle. They look adorable next to the tree topper.

I've placed a bottle of my new serum in every stocking, and they're full of questions about it. "I customized the ingredients for each of you," I explain, "and the base is Eunice's recipe."

"We'll need a line for the shop," Ruby states. "I'll design some labels."

"Whoa." I hold up my hands. "You better test them before we go that far."

Belle sniffs hers. "Does this have violet essential oil in it?"

"Would I make yours without your favorite scent?"

"It won't make my hair freak out, though, will it?"

I gently punch her arm.

She grins. "I knew you were cooking up wonderful things in the kitchen."

Ruby laughs. "Now we just have to work on your toast-making skills."

I toss a wadded up ball of paper at her. "I'll leave the food preparation to you and Matilda."

"You can cook?" Rissy asks, eyeing her sister.

Matilda lifts her chin. "I'm pretty good at it, actually."

She leaves off that fact about needing to put a spell on the stove in order not to burn anything, but hey, we all have our secrets.

A fresh round of gift-giving ensues when Finn, Leo, and Ren show up. They're followed by Nonni and Poppi.

The house is filled with laughter and conversation. I light two candles on the mantle in remembrance of Mom and Dad, and I swear I can feel them, and even Eunice, among us as we pull out board games to play. Belle retrieves several photo albums to show Rissy a few of our past Christmases.

"Your family is lovely," she says, staring at a group shot of us when Belle and I were only four. "Family can be tough, but also priceless."

Matilda raises a cup to her. "To Asgard, may it bring us bliss."

It's said as a salute, and Rissy returns the gesture, raising hers. "To Asgard."

Uncle Odin chimes in as well. "Asgard will bring us bliss."

They all drink and Belle and I exchange a look. Matilda has spiked the cider again.

"I'd like to stay a little longer," Rissy says to Matilda. "If that's all right with you."

Matilda mulls it over, staring at her beverage. She glances at Cinder across the way.

I, too, look at her and see her give a tiny nod.

I grin. "Our home is your home for as long as you'd like to stay."

Ruby comes over to stand behind Matilda. "We need help with the sales floor and online orders. You can work off your room and board that way."

"Yes," Belle says, grinning and clapping.

Rissy seems okay with the compromise, but she hesitates, catching Matilda's eye. "What say you, sister?"

Matilda sighs dramatically and rolls her eyes. "As long as you don't cause trouble and stay human."

"Human?" Belle's grin falls off her face. "As opposed to what?"

Matilda motions at Rissy to tell us. Now she rolls her eyes, looking a lot like our godmother when she does it. "I'm a shapeshifter. A cat."

Ruby chuckles. "Is that so?" She winks at me. "We happen to like shifters."

"Sure, when they're wolves," Matilda clarifies. "Savannah may not be happy about having another cat in the house."

As if she agrees, Savannah cries from her bed under Uncle Odin's chair. "So stay human," I tell Rissy, "and that won't be a problem."

"What's it like to be a cat?" Belle slides her seat closer to the woman. "I've always thought it would be fun!"

The two of them began an animated discussion of the pros and cons of claws and fur. Cinder shakes her head at me and I laugh.

That aside, it's a lovely time of slowing down to appreciate our family. In anticipation of Snow, Broden, and Robyn joining us for the afternoon, more chairs are brought into the living room, with an assortment of cookies, candies, and drinks, including some spiked eggnog, made by Matilda.

I text Sawyer to wish him a Merry Christmas and he asks if he can come over. When he arrives, I offer to take his jacket and get him a drink, but he says no. His grandmother has invited some of the quilting club ladies who don't have relatives over for an afternoon tea and cookie exchange. He's promised to be there by her side.

"I brought you this," he says, pulling out a gift bag from inside his coat. I lead him away from the commotion and into the kitchen. At the work table, I open it and pull out a small wooden angel, complete with a halo.

"She's beautiful." I admire the details he's put into the feathered wings, as well as her expressive face. Instead of long hair, hers is spiked, the halo tipped slightly sideways. 'Always a rebel,' is written in gold, the tiny letters hidden in the folds of the gown.

Tears sting my eyes as I glance up at him. "This may be my favorite gift ever."

He takes my hand, drawing me close. "I regret leaving with all of my heart. I never meant to hurt you. Believe me when I say, I truly thought you'd be better off without me. Yes, I left because I needed to take care of Mom, but along the way, I finally realized no one can fill that empty place inside her. She keeps searching for her soulmate, but in reality, none of those guys ever mean as much to her as I do. I didn't want to continue going through life choosing between you and her."

A tear spills over the edge of my lid and I swipe it away. "So what's changed?"

"I have. My mother is a very unique person, and I'm determined to be there for her when she needs me. I'm just as determined to make a life with you, Zelle. Don't ever doubt that."

As if the universe needs to test his commitment, his phone rings. My intuition isn't my strongest gift, but I immediately know who's on the other end. "Don't answer that," I whisper.

He doesn't.

Maybe Janice is simply calling to wish him a Merry Christmas, but when he leans in and kisses me, all thoughts of his mother vanish.

It doesn't last long enough and his lips are gone before my heart can totally embrace what's happening between us. "I have to run," he says, "but I'll be back."

I rejoin the group after he dashes off, soon welcoming the rest of our family, and helping to prepare our Christmas Day Sherwood meal.

Later that evening, I'm thoroughly stuffed and my cheeks ache from smiling so much. My happiness comes crashing down though when Sawyer calls.

"She's in Miami. Karl left her, the pig. Can you imagine, on Christmas of all days. She's all alone, Zelle. She begged me to come and get her."

For a long moment, I bite my lip so I don't say the

words that are on my tongue. Not many sons care for their mother the way he does, but here it is again—she's his Achilles' heel. No matter what he claims, he'll never get out from under her antics.

I swallow hard and find the most compassionate voice I have. "Go get her. Tell her Merry Christmas from me. Do you have any idea when you'll be back?"

"No," he says on a tired sigh, "but I *will* come home to you."

# TWENTY-THREE

Hours later, my sisters are all with their boyfriends, and Snow and Broden have gone home. Matilda, Rissy, and Uncle Odin sit around the dying fire, the entire house smelling of wood smoke.

It's quiet and I adjourn to the tower to be alone for a few minutes. Like Shelby the night before, I stare up at the stars. The tower is so high, I almost feel as if I'm in outer space and I could reach out and touch them if I wanted.

I feel the old familiar ache in my chest, wondering if there actually is a future for me and Sawyer. I dared hope there was, and now the rug has been pulled out from under me again.

"Make a wish," Rissy says from behind me.

I glance back and see her downing more of the spiked eggnog. "I don't know what to hope for anymore."

"What your heart desires."

I smirk. "Already tried that a bunch of times. Never seems to take."

She hands me a second mug. "Maybe you need a little magick."

I accept it, but don't drink. I crane my neck to peer down the street at the quilt shop. A few lights are on and I wonder if Minerva is alone. I should take some of this brew to her. "Tried that, too. I'm destined to be alone."

She chortles. "Sugar, you've got more friends and family than half this county by what I witnessed today. You're a lucky girl."

Sighing, I turn from the window, seeing a falling star from the corner of my eye. "You're right. I have my health, my family, and my magick. I am lucky."

I follow her downstairs and find Rumpel and Savannah vying for space on Uncle Odin's lap. He's half asleep, his bow tie askew. "It was a wonderful day," he says.

I sit next to Nonni, who's already planning her next quilt. She smiles and squeezes my arm. "You did good with that little girl and her family," she says.

Next to her, Poppi nods. "We're real proud of you."

My phone rings and I nearly fumble to answer it, hoping it's Sawyer. The caller ID reads *unknown number*. "Hello?"

Megan's voice is excited. "Merry Christmas, Zelle, I'm sorry to interrupt your day, but I just had to share some good news."

"What is it?"

"A miracle. Shelby's doctor got word back about her latest round of test results and..." her voice hiccups. "The cancer is gone. My baby is going to be all right!"

I bolt to my feet, pure joy flowing through me. "That's awesome. I'm so happy for you."

"Everyone has been pulling for her, and even though it's Christmas, the lab and her doctor made sure to get us the results today so we could celebrate. Shelby would like to talk to you."

"Of course!" I'm grinning from ear to ear. Everyone is eyeing me suspiciously, so I cover the speaker and whisper, "Shelby's been cured."

The girl comes on the phone. "Zelle? I really do believe in angels and Santa Claus. I know you're one of his elves, or maybe an angel, because this is the best Christmas ever! Connor got his spirit back. It's what I told Santa I wanted."

"Santa is one cool guy." I wink at Uncle Odin. "Don't ever forget that he loves you, and so do the angels. Tell Connor hello from me, will you?"

She giggles and the sound melts my heart. "I will. Thank you."

Megan comes back on and we discuss having coffee after the New Year.

After we disconnect, I fill the others in on the good news. There's a knock at the back door, and I go to answer. Sawyer is standing there with his grandmother.

"I know it's late," Minerva says, pushing her way in and hugging me. Sawyer is carrying several containers with cookies, and she has a bag in her hands. "But we needed to come and share our bounty."

"I thought you went to Miami?"

He hands me one of the carriers. "Mamaw and I discussed Mom, and..."

His grandmother sets down the bag and removes the scarf from around her neck, tossing it on the back of a chair. "That daughter of mine is done screwing up our lives. It's time she started figuring things out on her own."

Rumpelstiltskin jets in to see who's here. He hops up onto the chair and grabs the scarf, wrapping it around himself.

Sawyer gives a cheeky grin. "We sent her bus fare, and I told her she has to come to Story Cove if she wants to be a family again."

I throw my arms around his neck and he lifts me off the floor in a hug. "I love you," I blurt.

He laughs and sets me on my feet. "I love you, too, Rebel."

Minerva teases the ferret with a gentle tug of war. "What do I have to do to get some hot cocoa?"

In the kitchen, Nonni joins us. "Isn't this the merriest of times?" she asks, winking at me.

"Thought you might want to have this," Minerva says, handing her the quilt.

She shakes it out and we all admire it. The angel in

the center has a demure look on her face, her hair ribbons of gold, silver, and iridescent white. There are several woodland creatures at her feet, including a ferret whose face reminds me of another cutie. "Your mother started this the year you and Belle were born," she says to me. "I thought it would honor her memory to finish it for her."

I run my fingers over the binding. "It's absolutely beautiful and reminds me of the town angel."

Nonni smiles. "It's yours now, Zelle. She would want you to have it. Any time you miss her, wrap yourself in it, okay?"

I accept the beautiful memento, forcing myself not to cry, and hug my grandmother. "I can't thank you enough."

Minerva pats my back and she and Nonni rejoin the others, leaving me and Sawyer alone. He leans one hip on the corner of the table, pulling me between his knees. "I'm new to this," he says, fingering a lock of my hair that's currently striped red and green. "But I'm so relieved to be here with you and not on the road to Miami."

I study his face, soaking it up. "Ditto."

He taps his bicep. "Do you know why I got this tattoo?"

My heart is jumping around in my chest. The confession of love is doing funny things to me. "Duh. Because even though you tried, you couldn't get over me."

He chuckles and leans his forehead against mine.

"You'll always have my heart, no matter where I go or what I do."

I run my hands over his shoulders and down his arms, needing to feel him here, right now, with me. It's not a fantasy or a dream; this is real. "I'm glad you're here, but I do hope your mother uses that bus ticket. I don't want to come between you and her, ever."

"I love her, but she is more than I can handle. Mamaw had a stern talking to me about boundaries and she's right. I knew it before she even said anything, but old habits die hard, you know? That knight in shining armor gig is hard to give up."

"As an independent woman, I can assure you I don't need one."

He tucks a piece of my hair behind my ear. "I'm well aware, but I hope you'll have me, just the same."

The angel he made me is in my pocket. "You'll always be a hero in my book."

His shoulders relax. "I've known for some time that I have to stop being the parent in my relationship with my mom. She needs to grow up and take responsibility for herself. I'll help her as much as I can, but I have a life to lead, and that life is with you."

We're all maturing and changing, I realize, and yet we're coming back home to each other at the same time. "Healthy families morph and grow, and we choose how to change with them."

He touches my cheek. "Both our families are expanding, but our core connection is strong and will always be there, don't you think?"

My hair turns its natural shade, then glows with cascading layers of the rainbow. Now, I finally realize, it's a good thing. "I couldn't agree more. I can't wait to see what the New Year brings for all of us."

He smiles, tugging a box from his pocket. "I suspect we'll all live happily ever after."

"What is this?" I gasp as he opens it.

A large pink stone surrounded by diamonds sparkles at me. "It's morganite," he says, slipping it out. "I knew you wouldn't go for the traditional engagement ring, so I asked Belle, and she said this was your mother's favorite gemstone."

I cover my gaping mouth. "Belle knew about this?"

He laughs. "She told me I better do right by you or she'd put a hex on me. Told me to go over to Svenson's and pick out the biggest morganite they had. I figured she knew you better than anyone, so I did." My hand shakes as he takes it. "I've been in love with you since I was eleven. What are you doing next year on Christmas Eve?"

The rainbow colors slow and stripes of silver and gold bleed into them. "Getting married?"

"It's always been your dream, hasn't it? To marry on that day?"

My answer comes out rushed and giggly. "Yes."

He clears his throat and goes down on one knee, holding the ring near the appropriate finger on my left hand. "Zelle Sherwood, my rebel witch, will you marry me?"

I can't believe my dreams are coming true. I can't

bring my parents back, but they're always with me in my heart. Rumpel hops onto his knee and watches my face, as if he understands what's happening.

"What do you think?" I ask my ferret, giving his tiny head a pat. "No more blue Christmases for us, huh?"

He chitters and makes clapping motions with his front paws.

"What does that mean?" Sawyer asks.

"The ferret says we're a go," I laughingly tell him. Then I tug him to his feet, Rumpel jumping down and sitting at my ankles. "I'd be happy to marry you next Christmas Eve."

He grins. "It's a date."

Taking my long, magickal hair, I wrap a length of it around him and pull him in for a kiss.

# READY FOR MORE MAGICK?

**Don't miss the next exciting adventure!** Sign up for Nyx's Cozy Clues Mystery Newsletter.

**And check out these magical stories!**

**Sister Witches Of Raven Falls Mystery Series**

**Sister Witches of Raven Falls Special Collection**

*Of Potions and Portents*
*Of Curses and Charms*
*Of Stars and Spells*
*Of Spirits and Superstition*

**Confessions of a Closet Medium Cozy Mystery Series**

**Confessions of a Closet Medium Special Collection**

*Pumpkins & Poltergeists*
*Magic & Mistletoe*
*Hearts & Haunts*
*Vows & Vengeance*
*Cupcakes & Corpses*
*Tea Leaves & Troubled Spirits*

**Sister Witches of Story Cove (Formerly Once Upon a Witch) Cozy Mystery Series Coming Fall 2022**

Cinder
Belle
Snow
Ruby
Zelle

# ABOUT THE AUTHOR

USA Today Bestselling Author Nyx Halliwell who grew up on TV shows like *Buffy the Vampire Slayer* and *Charmed*.

She loves writing stories as much as she loves baking and crafting. She believes in magick and that we each carry it inside us.

She enjoys binge-watching mystery shows with her hubby and reading all types of stories involving magic and animals.

Connect with Nyx today and see pictures of her pets, be the first to know about new books and sales, and find out when Godfrey, the talking cat, has a new blog post! Receive a FREE copy of the Whitethorne Book of Spells and Recipes by signing up for her news-letter http://eepurl.com/gwKHB9

# CONNECT WITH NYX TODAY!

Website: nyxhalliwell.com

Email: nyxhalliwellauthor@gmail.com
Bookbub https://www.bookbub.com/profile/nyx-halliwell
Amazon amazon.com/author/nyxhalliwell
Facebook: https://www.facebook.com/NyxHalliwellAuthor/

Sign up for Nyx's Cozy Clues Mystery Newsletter and be the FIRST to learn about new releases, sales, behind-the-scenes trivia about the book characters, pictures of Nyx's pets, and links to insightful and often hilarious *From the Cauldron With Godfrey blog*!

# DEAR MAGICAL READER

I hope you enjoyed this story! If you did, and would be so kind, would you leave a review on Goodreads, Bookbub, or your favorite book retailer? I would REALLY appreciate it!

A review lets hundreds, if not thousands, of potential readers know what you enjoyed about the book, and helps them make wise buying choices. It's the best word-of-mouth around.

The review doesn't have to be anything long! Pretend you're sharing the story with a good friend. Pick out one or more characters, scenes, or dialogue that made you smile, laugh, or warmed your heart, and tell them about it. Just a few sentences is perfect!

Blessed be,

Nyx 🤍